'I hate you.'

'I know.' Raul dipped his head and nipped her earlobe. 'Imagine how incredible it will be… all that hate fuelling all that lust.'

Sensation filled Charley, every crevice of her coming alive at his touch, and at the whisper of his breath on her skin.

Two years without this…

Somehow she managed to pull her hands free from his grasp, fully intending to use them as weapons to push him off. Instead, working of their own accord, they hooked around his neck to pull him in for her hungry lips to connect with his. She had no sane comprehension of what she was doing. Instinct was taking over to seize what her body so desperately wanted.

In that instant any sort of rationality dissolved from her mind.

In a mesh of lips and tongues they came together, devouring each other, her fingers digging into his scalp, one of his hands sweeping up her back and nestling into her hair, clasping her head tightly.

His taste filled her and his warm breath merged with her own, sending deeper darts of need into her. Every part of her was aching for his touch, his kiss, his caress…

Michelle Smart's love affair with books started when she was a baby, when she would cuddle them in her cot. A voracious reader of all genres, she found her love of romance established when she stumbled across her first Mills & Boon® book at the age of twelve. She's been reading (and writing) them ever since. Michelle lives in Northamptonshire with her husband and two young Smarties.

Books by Michelle Smart

Mills & Boon® Modern™ Romance

The Russian's Ultimatum
The Rings That Bind

Society Weddings

The Greek's Pregnant Bride

The Irresistible Sicilians

What a Sicilian Husband Wants
The Sicilian's Unexpected Duty
Taming the Notorious Sicilian

**Visit the author profile page at
millsandboon.co.uk for more titles**

THE PERFECT
CAZORLA WIFE

BY
MICHELLE SMART

MILLS & BOON

ISBN: 978-0-263-25852-3

THE PERFECT
CAZORLA WIFE

This book is dedicated to Pippa, my wonderful editor.
Thank you for everything you do—
I couldn't do any of this without you.

CHAPTER ONE

THE MOONLIGHT THAT poured over the mountaintop hotel gave it an ethereal, mysterious quality. From one perspective it looked enticing, welcoming. From Charley's perspective, the shadows it cast spelled danger. The moonlight shouldn't be silver. It should be red.

But this was no time for imagined threats. She was here for one purpose and one purpose only.

Taking a fortifying deep breath, she waited for the barrier to rise then drove through and parked in the main car park. No valet approached to whisk her Fiat 500 off to the secure parking area filled with Ferraris, Lamborghinis, Maseratis and the like.

Ambient music greeted her in the sprawling lobby where hotel guests were lounging around in their finery sipping on pre- and post-dinner drinks. She didn't make eye contact with anyone, intent on slipping through to the function room at the back.

The closer her steps took her, the louder the thuds of her heart grew. By the time she reached the door, the beats inside her were so loud the ambient music was completely drowned out.

A barrel of a man materialised, preventing her entry into the room.

'Your invitation, please,' he said, holding out his hand.

'My husband arrived earlier,' she answered in hesitant

Spanish. She'd lived in the country for over five years but only in recent months did she feel she'd got an actual grip on the language. She still kept her phrasebook in her handbag just in case. 'He left word that I would be getting here late,' she lied.

'Your husband?'

Charley reached into her silver clutch bag, removed her passport and handed it over. 'Raul Cazorla.' She imagined how her soon-to-be ex-husband would react if he were in this situation and tried to channel some of his arrogance. She held her phone up. 'Would you like me to call him so he can come and verify who I am?'

She could see the guard debating what to do. No doubt he had taken Raul's invitation himself. No doubt he had clocked the flame-haired lingerie model on his arm too.

Thinking of that lingerie model...

A host of bitter feelings curdled in Charley's belly, just as they had two weeks ago when the first picture of the happy couple had been spread on the cover of one of Spain's high-end glossies. Raul had looked like the cat who'd licked the bowl dry of all the cream, which Charley supposed wasn't all that surprising. Physically, Jessica was perfect.

She doubted the model was his first lover since she'd left, just the first he'd publicly acknowledged.

Who he saw was none of her business, she reminded herself. In a few short weeks their divorce would be finalised. He would be a free agent.

She inhaled deeply and narrowed her eyes, little signs she had seen Raul perform hundreds of times to denote his displeasure at whatever situation was occurring. 'Perhaps you would prefer to find him yourself and ask him to confirm who I am?'

She knew her words had done the trick when the guard

placed his hand on the door to admit her. Who wanted to be the man to seek out Raul Cazorla, one of Spain's richest men, in the middle of a high-society party, to ask him if the woman bearing his name really was his wife?

'Enjoy the party,' he said, opening the door.

The function room of Barcelona's Hotel Garcia was a mass of glitz and silver and heaving with glamorous bodies. Unlike the easy jazz music of the lobby, here a DJ was playing a set, popular dance music throbbing beneath her already aching feet. It had been nearly two years since she'd last worn high heels and all the bones in her feet were protesting.

Waiters and waitresses armed with trays of champagne and *hors d'oeuvres* mingled discreetly, but close enough for Charley to swipe a flute of champagne and drink it in one swallow.

As she scoured the room she became aware of curious eyes watching her, imagined she could hear the whispers of, 'Is that Charlotte...?'

She tuned them out, focusing her attention on the open French doors that led out into the expansive gardens and the balmy night air.

The garden was alive with revellers sitting on the many iron tables and chairs scattered over the lawn, people talking, smoking, kissing...

Her heart recognised him first, accelerating to a gallop as she spotted the tall, muscular frame standing in the far distance, his back to her, a hand in his pocket. He was deep in conversation with a man she didn't recognise. On the table beside them sat two women chatting between themselves. The redhead took a long drag of a cigarette.

Raul hates smoking, she thought faintly.

For a horrible moment she thought she was going to be sick.

She'd barely taken a step when he turned his head as if sensing eyes upon him.

He tilted his face a touch in her direction then turned back to the gentleman he was talking to and carried on his conversation.

Gathering all her courage, Charley began to walk. She'd only taken a few steps when he turned his head again. This time his eyes fixed directly on her.

He twisted his body round fully to face her.

As she neared him he became more than just a figure in the distance. Step by step he seemed to expand and flesh out, becoming solid. Becoming Raul.

He was as handsome as her tortured mind remembered.

Dimly she noted the dark hair cropped short, the black bow tie loosened around his neck, the perfectly tailored handmade suit hugging his snake hips...

By the time she reached the table, all conversation between his companions had stopped. In particular, she could feel the redhead's eyes boring into her.

'Hello, Raul,' Charley said softly, the anger that had propelled her to gatecrash this party diminishing as she took in the face she had last seen in the flesh almost two years ago.

If her appearance shocked him, he hid it well. He'd always been able to hide his emotions well. Apart from in the bedroom...

'Charlotte,' he said, leaning forward to place a kiss on both her cheeks. 'This is an unexpected pleasure.'

At least, those were the words his mouth said. His eyes spoke a different tale. Even through the tingling on her cheek where his lips had met her skin, she could see the fire spitting from them.

When he next spoke she could hear the tightness of his vocal cords. 'Excuse me, Andres, ladies.' With those polite parting words, he bore her away, taking hold of her arm and clasping it tightly enough to prevent her escaping but not so hard as to hurt.

Eyes followed them as they walked in silence to the far corner of the garden, the part where discreet benches were placed amongst the blooming flowers for lovers to be alone. With every step she took, Charley forced her mind to concentrate, to remember the words she'd spent the day rehearsing.

Being here with him was a thousand times harder than she'd imagined it would be.

The last time she'd seen her husband had been exactly six hundred and thirty-three days ago.

The last time she'd seen her husband they'd been screaming at each other, real hate and fury spilling out like a bunch of fireworks detonating in one big bang. She'd left that night and hadn't seen him since.

She'd thought all the hurt and anger from that evening and everything that had led up to it had gone, that she was over it and moving on with her life. To feel the same maelstrom of emotions stirring within her scared her more than anything she'd experienced since that night.

She could feel him trying to rein in his own fury too, in subtle ways that only someone who'd been intimate with him for a long time would recognise. Someone like his wife.

Only when they were safely out of sight, hidden behind a cherry tree laden with fruit, did he drop her arm and glower down at her. 'What are you doing here, Charlotte?'

'I'm here to speak to you.'

'That much is obvious. The question is why have you wormed your way into this party when I've made it clear I have no wish to see you?'

His words shouldn't feel like a slap to the face. But they

did. They stung as badly as his refusal to take her calls and as badly as when he'd cancelled the appointment she'd made to see him less than an hour after his PA had put it in his diary. Charley had heard the mortification in Ava's voice when she'd called her back with the bad news.

'I need your help,' she said with a helpless shrug, gazing intently into the pale blue eyes she'd once adored. The very first time she'd caught a glimpse of him it had felt as if her heart expanded enough to consume the rest of her. The high cheekbones, the full lips offset by a firm jaw…

She blinked and looked away. Raul's intense masculinity that bordered on beauty had turned her brain to mush before. She needed to keep her head together, not plunge back five years to a time when her libido did her thinking for her. This was her one chance to convince him to help her. 'Did you get my letter and the finance report I put with it?'

His throat emitted a sound of disgust. 'Are you talking about the begging letter I received a couple of days ago?'

She rubbed an eye and immediately wished she hadn't. She'd spent an *age* applying her make-up, unpractised after almost two years of not wearing it, and in one frustrated rub had probably ruined it. But she needed to look the part, not just to gain access to the party but to convince Raul to take her pleas seriously. Image was everything to her estranged husband. Regardless of what occurred behind closed doors, the public face had to be perfect.

'So you've read it?'

Raul had taken one look at the girlish handwriting on the envelope and known immediately who it was from. Charley's writing was undeveloped, as if she were stuck at age twelve.

It suddenly struck him that her handwriting was something she'd always been embarrassed about. She must have been really desperate to get in touch with him in this manner.

At the time he'd received her letter, though, he hadn't been thinking of anything like that. Seeing her handwriting there before him had hit him low in his gut, churning up so many emotions he'd screwed the envelope into a tight ball and thrown it at the wall. A good hour had passed before he'd retrieved it and taken a look at the content of her letter. He'd barely got a third of the way through before screwing it back up again. The finance report—and he used that term loosely—had gone straight in the shredding pile.

'I read enough to know you're after more of my money.' He'd transferred ten million euros into her account not long after she'd left, a reminder to her of everything she was giving up. He'd fully expected her to come crawling back. He'd *still* been expecting her to come crawling back a year later when the divorce papers had landed on his doorstep.

But now those millions had dried up and here she was, dressed to the nines, trying to get her greedy hands on more.

'I'm not after your money. Did you read the bit about the Poco Rio day care centre?'

'Yes.' It was as far as he'd got before the words had blurred in his eyes.

Poco Rio day care centre. Those five words had been the reason his hands had fisted the letter into a ball the second time. It had been his estranged wife's refusal to have a child with him that had killed their marriage.

He'd pumped an endless supply of money into her failed business ventures and now she had the nerve to ask him for money to fund yet another business, this one involving children, when she'd strung him along for three years with the promise of one.

He'd never thought of her as a sadist.

'Then you know how important this is. I've found the ideal premises but the owner won't hold onto them for ever. Either I complete the sale in the next month or he's pulling out. Please, Raul, there isn't time to find new premises. We've got four months left until we're kicked out of our current home and—'

'None of this concerns me. This is *your* problem.'

'But I'm running out of time! The place I've found is perfect. The grounds are enormous and, once all the renovations are done, the building itself will be ten times better than the one we're currently in and we'll be able to double the number of children.'

'As I said, this is your concern, not mine.'

'But without you I can't get the rest of the funding. I've tried everything…'

'Then try harder. Maybe this time you'll actually see something through to the end rather than giving up halfway through.'

She sucked in her cheeks at his home truth but met his gaze head-on. 'I won't give up this time. I *can't*. But no one's prepared to invest.'

'Then either your business plan needs working on or you need to change your résumé. Maybe you should consider changing the truth into lies and hope no one bothers to check it.' He backed away and nodded his head. 'I've given you enough of my time—my date will be feeling neglected. I trust you can see yourself out?'

She blanched at the mention of his date.

He waited for gratification to hit him but all he felt was something akin to guilt, although why that should be the case he couldn't begin to fathom. Charley had left *him*. After three years of his lavishing his money on her, helping her to improve herself, supporting her, giving her everything she desired…she'd refused him a child.

After three years of stringing him along, dangling the promise of a child over his head, she'd finally admitted the truth. She didn't want to have his baby.

Their whole marriage had been a lie, reduced to nothing but a cauldron of recrimination and hate.

And now she had the nerve to ask for his help.

Yet, staring at her now, her skin as pure as alabaster under the moonlight, Raul had to clench his hands into fists and hold them tightly to his sides to prevent them reaching out to touch her.

The first time he'd met her, he'd just taken over the running of the Cazorla Hotel chain, the family business run by his father until he'd suffered a major stroke. Despite having his own successful, unconnected business to run, Raul had stepped up to the plate and taken over. The stroke had left his father physically disabled and unable to speak but he'd perfectly conveyed the disgust he felt at this occurrence. Raul had known it was the thought of *him* taking over rather than his new physical situation his father had hated the most. He knew his father despised the roaring success he'd made of the business since.

Back then, he'd been in Majorca to inspect the Cazorla hotel there, as he'd done in turn with the whole chain, refamiliarising himself with the business. This hotel had been markedly different from the others, having turned into a family hotel over the years rather than a luxury resort as the others in the chain were famous for. Charley had been employed by an outside Spanish company as one of the entertainers there.

He'd first seen her late in the evening, leaving the complex, dressed in shorts, a shimmering top and flip-flops, long honey-blonde hair flowing around her shoulders.

She'd been laughing at something a friend had said, a deep, throaty laugh without inhibition that had made him smile to hear it. He'd spotted her again the next evening. She'd been on the stage running a game show that involved audience participation. She'd been funny and energetic and had the guests, young and old alike, eating out of her hand. He'd sought her out when the show finished, about to head out with her colleagues to party the rest of the night away. It hadn't taken much persuasion to get her to change her plans and join him instead.

Appearancewise, she couldn't have been more different from how she looked now in her expensive tight red dress with the plunging neckline that showcased her creamy cleavage and matching red heels. As soon as she'd been given access to his bank account, her style had changed dramatically, her wardrobe suddenly full of impeccable designer items.

Tonight, her long, thick hair had been dyed a warm blonde but he had no doubt it would be a different colour in a few weeks. Her hair changed more frequently than her ever-shifting career choices.

Her perfectly made up green eyes blinked rapidly as she pulled her generous lips into a tight white line. She reached out an imploring hand before quickly letting it drop. 'You're the only one who can help me. I've finally found a bank prepared to invest in the project but they'll only give me the rest of the funds if you act as guarantor.'

'What the...?' He bit away the oath that jumped on his tongue and glared at her, ignoring the plea ringing from her eyes. 'That's even worse than asking me for money outright. You must be mad if you think I would guarantee money on any business venture you embarked on. After all, I threw away millions of euros during our marriage on your failed ventures—'

A thought occurred to him. 'Why would the bank manager request I act as your guarantor? We've been separated for two years. Our divorce, which I remind you has come at *your* instigation, will be finalised in a few weeks.'

Her teeth sank sharply into her bottom lip and she cast her eyes down in a decidedly shamefaced manner. 'I…'

'What did you do?' His wife was nothing if not impulsive. She could have done anything.

'I…I told him we'd got back together.'

'You did *what*?'

She met his gaze with a cringe. 'I didn't know what else to do…'

'Let me get this straight—you told a bank manager we were back together so you could get investment on your latest hare-brained project?'

'It is *not* hare-brained,' she protested hotly, displaying the first real hint of fire since she'd gatecrashed the party. 'Without the funding, the children have nowhere to go.'

'That is *not* my problem.' The anger that had been simmering within him pushed to the surface. 'I don't care what lies you've told, I want nothing to do with it and nothing to do with you. This is your mess and your responsibility to sort out. Goodbye.'

Leaving her standing there open-mouthed, he strode away. He hadn't got more than a few metres before she called out to him.

'It isn't too late for me to sue for a slice of your fortune, you know.'

He came to an abrupt halt.

Now the truth of this meeting was revealed.

'Our divorce isn't final yet. I can call my lawyer Monday morning and tell him I've changed my mind and now want the large settlement he said I could have.'

Slowly he turned to face her, heart thundering, his brain burning. She dared to *threaten* him?

He did not take threats from anyone, especially not the woman who'd shared his bed for three years and milked him for everything she could before walking out on him.

'Yes, you can call your lawyer and, yes, a court will probably compel me to give you some of what you ask for. I've always been generous with you—it was your choice not to ask for more than I'd already given.' He'd been suspicious to find she didn't want more of his wealth than the ten million euros. Probably she'd seen all the zeros in her account and assumed it would last for ever. He was surprised it lasted as long as it had.

Somehow he found himself right back in front of her with no memory of his legs having moved.

'Any court case will take months, if not years, to settle so will come too late to save your latest business.' He allowed himself a smile as he leaned down to place his face inches from hers so she could follow his lips and their meaning more closely. 'In the meantime, you will have ample time to consider the folly of your extravagant ways and the consequences of your lies.'

This time he walked away without her calling him back.

As he rejoined the party the sight of her hurt, shocked face played heavily on his mind.

His date, Jessica, stared at him coolly, taking a long drag of her cigarette. 'What was that about?'

He looked at her. They'd been dating for almost a month, his first foray into the dating world since Charley had walked out.

Jessica was tall, lithe and beautiful, regularly featuring at the top of sexiest women polls. She was poised, cool and considered, and looked fantastic on his arm.

Charley was inches shorter and considerably curvier.

She was warm and impulsive with a laugh that warmed you to hear it. She smelled of fresh vanilla.

He could still smell her now.

'Well?' Jessica demanded, crunching her cigarette out in the ashtray.

Charley had always smelled gorgeous, especially first thing in the morning when the vanilla had turned to musk and mingled with the scent of their night's lovemaking.

He *hated* the smell of smoke. Was it any wonder he'd been loath to even kiss Jessica?

A dart of red crossed the periphery of his vision. He turned his head to see Charley hurry back into the hotel. Even from this distance he could see the dejection in her demeanour.

Forcing a smile at Jessica, he ignored her question. 'One more drink and then we'll make a move.'

Not giving her the chance to respond, he headed back into the hotel and the heaving function room. As he fought his way to the bar, bypassing the waiting staff and their trays of champagne—he needed something much stiffer than *that* to drink—he kept an eye out for a vision in red but she was nowhere to be seen.

Charley had gone.

CHAPTER TWO

CHARLEY FORCED A polite smile and an even politer *adiós*, and left the bank manager's office. Her chest felt so tight she struggled to breathe. Swallowing in a vain attempt to open her airways, she stepped into the lobby of the enormous building that housed her bank and a dozen other institutions, and headed straight to the ladies' room, locking herself in the nearest cubicle.

It was over.

The manager had been as good as his word. Without Raul to act as guarantor, there would be no loan.

She'd known her chances of getting the manager to change his mind had been slim but had refused to be defeated. Slim was a better chance than zero.

And now it was all over. That last glimmer of hope had died. Zero chance had become reality.

Clamping a hand over her mouth, she stifled a sob.

Despite all her efforts, Poco Rio would lose its home and close.

Those poor children. Whatever she felt was nothing in comparison to how it would affect them and their families. God alone knew they'd already suffered enough in their short lives.

She had to hold her hands up and admit defeat. There were no avenues left to explore. She'd done everything she could, even turning to Raul for help.

Another sob formed in her throat as she recalled how he'd thrown her desperate plea back in her face. She'd never have believed he could be so heartless, had had no idea he was still harbouring the fury that had underpinned the end of their marriage. Then, his fury, his loss of control, would have been frightening if her own anger hadn't matched his.

How clearly she remembered the reasonable tone he'd always adopted when discussing her failings. '*Cariño*,' he'd said, 'it is time for you to accept you are not business-minded. You have tried but now it is time for us to make the family we once talked of having.'

She remembered even more clearly how her blood, her skin, her bones—every part of her—had chilled at his words.

Bring a baby into this marriage?

Up until that point, having children was something she'd looked forward to having but in the future, after she'd found her niche in life.

Her own mother had worked hard to put food in Charley's belly. The fact she'd thrown away all her mum's hard work in her teenage years was something she'd become deeply ashamed of and determined to rectify. When she had a child of her own, she wanted her baby to look up to her. She didn't want her own children comparing their parents and seeing a father who was a roaring success and a mother who was a dismal failure. She wanted her husband and children to be proud of her, to see her as a successful woman in her own right.

It hadn't been on her mind to leave him but when she'd tried to explain why this still wasn't the right moment to have a baby, everything had turned on its head and somehow they'd been in each other's faces, shouting words she no longer remembered in detail but remembered the meaning behind.

Gold-digger and *failure* were two of his choice accusations that still rang clear and still had the power to make her stomach contract with pain. Those accusations had hurt terribly. She'd tried so *hard* to make a success of those businesses, had been desperate to impress him with something other than her body. But she had reached too high, she could see that now. Desperation had clouded her judgement; she had reached the stage where she couldn't see the wood for the trees. The trees had become so thick she couldn't see a way out either.

And then he'd told her to leave.

It had been like a light bulb going off in her skull. All the things she'd been in denial about had come to the forefront and with them had come the realisation that she couldn't do it any more. She couldn't be the woman he'd tried to shape her into being.

By the time she'd finished packing, he'd calmed down enough to tell her, not ask her, that he wanted her to stay. But it had been too late. Raul wanted perfection and she was far from perfect. She'd known as clearly as she knew her own name that their marriage was dead.

So why did she feel so heartsick to think about him? Why did she feel not just upset that he'd thrown her pleas for help back at her but a bone-deep misery that had stopped her eating more than a slice of toast since the party two days ago?

Only when she was certain she could keep the threatening tears at bay long enough to return home did Charley leave the ladies' room, making sure a smile lay on her lips. That was one of the things the decorum tutor Raul had employed had drilled into her: always show a pleasant demeanour whatever the circumstances. Image was everything to the Cazorlas.

Her head ached, hurting much worse than the time she'd swallowed too large a lump of ice cream and got brain-freeze. The brilliant Valencian sunshine magnified it and she shielded her eyes as she stepped outside.

Her car was parked around the corner but before she could walk to it her vision cleared and she made out the tall figure leaning against an illegally parked silver Lotus at the front of the building, arms crossed over his broad chest.

'Raul?'

For a moment she was too stunned to move or say anything else.

Seeing him in full daylight, gorgeous in a dark blue suit and light blue shirt that made the colour in his eyes gleam, threatened to knock what little stuffing she had left out of her heart.

This wasn't a coincidence. It couldn't be. Over the years Raul had wined and dined all the major players of the Spanish banks. He had all the best contacts. His web covered everywhere.

He'd probably known the outcome of her meeting before she had.

Suddenly it became clear what he was here for.

She marched over to him. 'Here to gloat, are you?'

He unfolded his arms and straightened, his pale blue eyes fixed on her without expression.

'No, *cariño*.' The faintest of smiles tugged at his sensuous lips. 'I'm here to offer you a lifeline.'

She studied him carefully, trying to read his face.

'What kind of lifeline?' she asked, not hiding her wariness.

'The kind of lifeline that will save your centre.'

Raul watched a dozen emotions flitter over her pretty face as she digested his words.

'You're going to help me?'

He allowed himself another smile and opened the passenger door of the Lotus. 'Get in and we'll discuss the matter.'

'Tell me where to go and I'll meet you. I've got my own car here.'

She could drive now? That was news to him.

'If you want the lifeline for the centre that means so much to you, I suggest you get in. This is a one-off discussion. When I leave, the offer of my help leaves with me.' Not waiting for a reaction, he sidled round and got into the driver's side.

It was only when he shut his door and fastened his seat belt that Charley galvanised herself into action, jumping in beside him and shutting the passenger door with a slam.

He put his sunglasses on before turning to face her, taking stock of the designer black suit she wore and the way her hair hung loose around her shoulders. It surprised him to find her make-up-free bar a touch of eyeliner and mascara. His wife normally made her face up so artfully that not the slightest imperfection showed; at least she had after she'd been given access to his bank account and had hit the high-class department stores. When he'd first met her she'd been as fresh-faced as she was today.

His loins tightened as he caught her vanilla scent. He'd been imagining that scent since she'd gatecrashed the party.

She stared right back at him, confusion and suspicion vying in her look.

He experienced a surge of satisfaction.

He had her exactly where he wanted her.

With a half-smile on his face, he shifted the car into gear and joined the rest of the traffic on the street.

'Are you serious about helping me?' she asked in the throaty tone he remembered so well.

'Why else would I be here?'

On Saturday night, his only intention had been to let her stew in the mess of her own making and get on with his life.

Charley had left him. She was nothing but a gold-digger who'd played him for a fool. She deserved *nothing*.

He'd dropped Jessica home after the party and returned to his own house alone, just as he'd slept alone since Charley had left him.

He'd lain awake, his mind drifting back to the nights he'd spent with his wife, remembering the curves of her body, the softness of her skin, the scent of their sex…for the first time in two years, his libido had awoken.

One short, angry conversation with his wife and his body—every part of it—had come back to life in a way it hadn't in the whole of their two years apart.

He'd recalled their conversation in minute detail, over and over, Charley vivid behind his eyes. He couldn't block her out.

When the sun came up he'd still been lying there, his mind still racing in a hundred different directions.

Not caring that it was a Sunday morning and that they would likely be in bed, he'd used his contacts to learn more about the finances behind her venture, including speaking to a businessman she'd pitched to.

He learned Charley only had the personal funds to pay for half the building costs. He dreaded to think what she'd blown the rest of the money he'd given her on.

Financially, her name was toxic. No investor would

touch her. Her own bank wouldn't touch her without his name as guarantor.

She'd explored all other avenues and now it was down to him and him alone to save her project.

Well, she would damn well pay the price for it, starting today.

'You're going to lend me the money?'

'Better than that—I'm going to give it to you.'

He let that sink in, letting her realise in her own sweet time that he alone had what was needed to make her dream a reality.

'Are you seriously serious?'

He almost laughed. He'd forgotten the way she had with words. 'Yes.'

'I'm assuming this offer comes with a catch.'

'Nothing in life comes free, *cariño*.' He felt her bristle at the use of his old name for her. Good. By the end of the day she would be doing a lot more than bristling beside him. By the time the sun went down she would be back in his bed beneath him.

Celibacy had not been a conscious decision. It was only as he'd lain in his bed thinking about her that he'd realised why he'd not found another bedmate.

How could he be with another woman when his wife still lived in his blood?

Charley hadn't just gatecrashed the party, she'd gatecrashed her way straight back under his skin. And he knew just the way to exorcise her once and for all.

'What's your catch?'

'We will discuss the terms when we get home.'

'You're taking me to Barcelona?'

'*Sí*. And when we get to my home we will share a civilised lunch and discuss the terms of the deal in detail. For now, you can rest your mind knowing that if you agree to my terms, the building you want to buy will be a done deal.'

Charley bit into her bottom lip and balled her hands into fists, digging her nails into the palms of her hands. If her nails were as long as she'd kept them when she'd been with Raul, she would have inflicted pain upon herself. Now they were short and practical and produced only the dullest of aches. Nowhere near enough to distract from the turmoil playing in her belly.

'Can you at least tell me why you changed your mind about helping me?'

'We will discuss everything when we get home.'

She wanted to demand answers but forced herself to think rationally. Right now he was being cordial towards her, his attitude a marked improvement to the loathing he hadn't bothered to hide at the party. He was here and, if he was as good as his word, prepared to help her. At that moment, that was all that mattered. Anything else she could worry about later. Antagonising him would accomplish nothing.

If she had to suffer his company then for the children's sake she would gladly accept it.

Her head might term it as suffering, but her body had a different word for the reaction provoked by being in the close confines of the car with him. It was familiar torture: her lungs tight, her pulse loose, her skin alive with awareness.

She breathed out slowly and peeked at him from the corner of her eye. Her heart swelled to see his sleeves rolled up, his tanned left arm resting on the ledge of the open window. Unlike most people with his wealth, Raul preferred to drive himself unless he was drinking. The first of his birthdays that they'd celebrated together, she'd bought him a day's racing at a racetrack. He'd been too well-bred to tell her he'd already raced on it a dozen times, happy that she'd bought something that actually meant something to him.

They'd been happy then. *She'd* been happy then.

She blinked the memories away and fixed her gaze on the road ahead.

A few minutes later they were at the heliport where his pilot awaited them, ready to take them back to Barcelona.

Charley stared up at Raul's home with a definite sense of awe and trepidation.

'When did you move in here?' she asked.

'A year ago,' came the curt reply.

In direct contrast to the old villa, which had been set in a private enclave by the beach, Raul's new villa was located in the exclusive neighbourhood of Avenida Tibidabo. Surrounded by high-security gates that in turn were lined with palm trees, the villa was three-storey, with cream outer walls and turrets, all topped with terracotta roofs.

Intuition told her she was walking into a trap, although she couldn't fathom what it could be. Once she knew exactly what he wanted from her she'd deal with it. It was the not knowing that made her feel so tense, that and being back in the company of the man whose masculinity she'd always found so very potent. It shamed her that even now, after so much water had passed beneath the bridge, her body was as alert to him as it had always been.

The villa's differences internally were as marked as the location. The home they'd shared by the beach, although just as grand, had been modern. This villa was steeped in splendour, with mosaicked floors and high, arched frescoed ceilings, a sense of history breathing through the whitewashed walls.

Here was the evidence, if she hadn't already guessed it by his two years of silence, that Raul had moved on.

She swallowed the acrid taste that had formed in the back of her throat. 'Where are the staff?' At this time of day the house should be teeming with activity, especially on a Monday.

'I told the household staff to take the day off.' Raul's eyes gleamed with something she couldn't interpret. 'I thought it best for us to be alone.'

Low, down in the juncture of her thighs, heat pulsed and licked through her veins.

How *could* she still react to him like that, as if the past two years had never happened?

She rubbed her arms, her trepidation growing with each passing second. 'What are the terms you want to talk about? Only, I'm working at the centre tomorrow and want to get back to Valencia before it gets late.'

'We can talk while we eat.'

She followed him through to a dining room with huge windows that looked out onto the villa's gardens. The sun shone down, beaming on the manicured lawn and the abundance of flowers and shrubs.

A long dark wood table had been set for two. Raul pulled a chair out for her. 'Lunch has been prepared for us. Make yourself at home.'

Home? She gagged at the thought. This would never be her home. In a few weeks they would be officially divorced. She was almost counting the days.

She sat gingerly, running her fingers over the silver cutlery in silent contemplation.

Any moment now and his real motive for bringing her here would be revealed. She doubted it was to do with the money. Unlike Charley, who'd proven herself to be a spectacular failure in business, her husband had a habit of turning whatever he touched into gold. Much as she tried to avoid reading media reports on him, it was like telling a child not to touch the nice shiny toy in the corner. Already worth hundreds of millions, he'd sold the technology firm he'd founded and run before his father's stroke had forced him to take over the running of the Cazorla luxury hotel chain. The sale had earned him a reported two and a half billion euros. Since taking over the family firm he'd added a fleet of aeroplanes and half a dozen brand spanking new cruise liners to the stable.

Simply speaking, her husband was worth more than entire countries.

If she'd taken her lawyer's advice she could have taken a good slice of his wealth, far exceeding the ten million he'd transferred into her account without consulting her. She hadn't wanted to take even that, had left it untouched for months. It was Raul's money, not hers. She'd contributed nothing to it so why should she have a claim to it?

She'd spent enough of his money during their marriage as it was.

He came back into the dining room carrying a platter of antipasto: deli meats, marinated vegetables, roasted peppers and sundried tomatoes, olives, cheese, rustic breads… all her favourite bites. And to think this was only the first course…

He poured her a glass of the red wine that had been left to breathe on the table, then raised his glass in a toast before swallowing half his wine and taking the seat beside her.

Charley couldn't bear it a moment longer. 'This all looks delicious and I thank you, but I can't eat anything until you tell me what your terms are.'

Helping himself to a little of everything before them, Raul took a bite of some bread then fixed his eyes on her as he ate. Once he'd swallowed and taken another drink of his wine, he answered. 'I am prepared to give you the money you need to buy the building and for all the renovations that will be needed to make the day care centre fit for purpose.'

She returned his stare, waiting for the catch that was surely coming.

'When do you have to get the renovations done by?' he asked. 'Four months, was it?'

'Yes. The new owners agreed to give us six months to relocate.' She watched him with caution. 'Two of those months have already gone.'

The owner of the building that housed Poco Rio had died unexpectedly, leaving the team who worked there rudderless. Worse still, his family had not shared his sentimentality and opted to sell to a developer, only telling the staff about it when it was a done deal.

'Four months to complete the purchase and the renovations?'

'It sounds like a long time but it isn't. We need to make it as safe and as suitable for the children's needs as it can possibly be. Walls need to be knocked down, doorways need to be extended...'

Raul made a dismissive motion with his hand. 'All of that can be discussed when we have reached an agreement.'

'But what is it you want me to agree to?' she asked in bewilderment. 'The centre receives sufficient funds to repay any loan.'

His lips curved upwards. It was like looking at a sensuous shark. 'As I said earlier, I will not be giving you a loan. With your track record, who knows when I will get it back?'

Her ire, already simmering at his mocking attitude, rose. 'I already told you...'

'You have the business acumen of a child. I trust your figures as much as I trust your judgement.'

'My judgement must have been seriously off when I married *you*.'

She regretted her hotly spat words before they'd left her tongue. So much for not antagonising him until the deal was done.

Raul's smile remained but his eyes had turned to ice. 'It is a shame you feel that way but it's not a sentiment I happen to share.

'When I say *giving* I do not mean it in the literal sense. I *will* require a form of payment but not one of monetary value.'

She'd known it. From the minute she'd got into his car she'd known there was a catch involved.

'My condition for giving you the money and for giving your project all the skills and expertise at my disposal is modest. I want you back in my bed and living with me as my wife until the work on the new building is complete.'

CHAPTER THREE

THE COLOUR DRAINED so quickly from Charley's face that Raul braced himself to steady her should she faint.

Then the colour returned, her cheeks staining a dark, angry red.

'What do you mean, *live as your wife*? We're getting a divorce.'

'Which we can put on hold.' Deliberately he drained his wine. 'If you want this new home for the centre, then that's the payment I require.'

'But *why*? Of all the things you could want, why that? Until Saturday night we hadn't spoken in almost two years. Our marriage is dead.'

'Our divorce isn't finalised.' He swallowed a plump black olive. 'We will put it on hiatus until the renovation work is complete and the centre reopened.'

'I don't see why that means we have to pretend to be back together.'

'There won't be any pretence about it. But to answer your question, I will be donating a considerable amount of money to your project and I want to be there to make sure you don't give up on it halfway through.'

'I would never do that.'

'You founded three different businesses in our time to-gether. They all failed because you lost interest, failed to take the good advice I gave you, and let things slip. I won't just be backing this project; I'll be taking control of it.'

She winced at his cold assessment of her failures but understood his meaning immediately. 'You haven't the faintest idea what the project entails or what's needed for the renovations.'

'You will be by my side to assist me. Think of it as a learning curve. Four months to learn how to run a business properly rather than rely upon guesswork. After all,' he continued, 'it won't be my bank balance that suffers if you fail but the children and families you've made promises to.'

More angry colour flooded her cheeks. Her green eyes darkened, her fury as easy to read as a book.

He refused to feel any sympathy.

Charley loved children. He'd seen that from the first. They'd discussed starting a family of their own and he'd shown great patience in her request that they wait a few years so she could make something of herself first.

He'd lavished her with everything she desired.

In return she'd denied him what *he* desired: the baby she'd promised.

Together they would have created the perfect family.

He'd imagined their unborn child a thousand times, imagined how different a parent he would be from his own father. Not for his child the feeling of being worthless. His children's achievements would be celebrated, their failures whether minor or major understood and forgiven, their opinions valued. He would have shown his father what being a father was *really* about. It was everything his father hadn't been.

'Take control of the project if you must,' Charley said, a tremor racing through her voice. 'Be the big alpha man you are and throw your weight and money around as you always do. So long as the centre reopens in four months' time I don't care how it's done, but there is no need to go through a charade of us being back together.'

He clenched his hands into fists, straining not to react to her inflammatory words. Taking control of situations where he was the most suitable person to take charge was not akin to throwing his weight around. She made him sound like a tyrant, which, he was certain, was deliberate. His wife might be uneducated but she was not stupid. Regardless, he would keep his cool even if she couldn't.

'I fail to see what your issue is,' he said, channelling his composure. 'You were happy to tell your bank manager the barefaced lie that we're back together when it suited you. This arrangement suits *me* but in this case it will not be a lie. For four months you will live with me as my wife and then you will be free to resume your life. But this time our marriage will end on *my* terms.'

Already he could taste the satisfaction that would bring. It might even taste as sweet as having his wife back in his bed.

The wildness he'd sensed in her from that first look had translated into the bedroom. Making love to her had always been out of this world. Whether it was hard and fast or slow and sweet, their passion for each other had been unquantifiable.

'This is your pride talking, isn't it? Because I had the nerve to leave you? You want to humiliate me?'

'Not at all,' he answered with deliberate smoothness, counteracting the vibrations emanating from her delectable frame. A charge flickered through his loins to see her face become the same colour it rose to when in the throes of passion. 'You want my help and I'm prepared to give it to you but in return I want payment—and the only form of payment you are in a position to make is with your body.'

She pushed her chair back as if she'd been scalded and got to her feet. 'You want me to prostitute myself?'

'I'm merely requesting that you, my wife, return to the

marital bed for a fixed period and in that period you make yourself available to me wherever and whenever I require.'

The charge in his loins tightened at the thought of her doing whatever pleased him. All those years when he'd done everything in his power to please her, in bed and out...now the tables had turned and it was her subjugation he required. For a limited time.

Yes, four months should serve him perfectly. During their marriage they'd spent a substantial amount of time apart, the distance always stoking the flames of lust so when they were together they made the most of every minute. This time, he would keep her by his side continuously so the lust they shared would finally be slaked and he could walk away from her without a backwards glance. Just as she had walked away from him.

Charley's legs felt wobbly. *Everything* felt wobbly. She hadn't touched a morsel of food, knew she wouldn't be able to swallow it past her throat.

'In all the years I've known you, I've never hated you.' Her body trembling, she forced her eyes to keep their gaze on his cool, unflinching stare. 'I hate you right now, more than I thought it was possible to hate another human being.'

He rose and, although he smiled down at her, his eyes were like ice. 'I don't care for your hate any more than I care for your love.' He reached out a hand and slipped it under the open top buttons of her blouse to rest on her collarbone.

She didn't want to react to the feel of his warm fingers on her skin...

She held her breath, his touch setting off a charge within her, certain he must be able to feel the hammering of her heart.

It was the first time he'd touched her in so, *so* long.

His voice dropped to a murmur. 'I am willing to give

you what you want. Are you willing to give me what *I* want? Because, let us speak frankly, it's the only thing you're any good at.'

If his thumb hadn't found the exact spot on her neck that always sent tingles of need and delight rippling through her, Charley might have reacted to his words a little quicker. As it was, it took a few moments for them to sink in and when they did she wrenched his hand away and pushed at his chest.

'How dare you reduce me to nothing but a plaything? I'm not a sex toy.'

The ice in his eyes melted into a gleam, as if he'd accepted a challenge. He reclosed the gap between them, trapping her against the table. 'You never had a problem being my sex toy before.'

Heat streamed through her at the feel of him pressed against her, all the memories she'd spent six hundred and thirty-five days trying to forget pouring into her mind.

She had lusted after him from their first conversation.

He'd been like no one she'd met before. Outrageously handsome, ridiculously wealthy…everything a young woman of twenty could wish for in a man. Prince Charming had come to life and it was *her* slipper he wanted. Was it any wonder her head had been turned?

And the sex… Never had she imagined such carnal responses existed within her, the same responses that were flashing back to life now, at the time when she needed her head clear to deal with what he was demanding of her.

It had been her own misfortune that she'd mistaken lust for love and married him. What they'd shared should never have been more than a summer fling.

As hard as she'd tried to fit in—and she'd tried *so* hard—she didn't belong in his world. She was a badly educated south-east London girl; elocution lessons paid for by her husband had knocked most of her mild cockney accent out of her. She'd come from a broken family where finances were erratic. Raul had grown up with wealth and social standing and had all the arrogance such an upbringing instilled.

They couldn't have been more wrong for each other if they'd got a computer program to determine their worst matches.

But the computer would have got their desire for each other right.

'That was when I loved you,' she said hoarsely. For love *had* grown from the lust, a greater love than she'd ever imagined could exist. Leaving him had been easy. Staying away had been almost unbearable.

And now that love had twisted into hate. But the desire was still there, however deeply she'd thought she'd buried it. 'If you ever felt anything for me you wouldn't ask for such a…a *despicable* thing from me.'

'Oh, I still feel a great deal for you.' He swept his fingers up her neck, pressing even closer.

She smothered the gasp that wanted to break out at the feel of his hardness against her.

Take control, Charley. Don't show your weakness for him.

'You can't force me.' The words she'd intended to come out forcefully were expelled with a whisper. Every inhalation brought *him* into her tight lungs, that masculine smell that had become as familiar to her as the scent of her home.

Her body remembered. His scent made it sing with delight.

He laughed softly into her ear and traced his fingers up her side. 'I don't need to force you.'

As if proving his point, he cupped her breast over her blouse and ran a thumb over a nipple straining against the suddenly restrictive bra she wore. The heat that had pooled low within her deepened, and she pressed her thighs together in denial.

He could demand all he wanted, but she would never give herself to him willingly, not now he was showing his true colours, the colours her love-blinded eyes had forgiven for far too long.

Mortified at her lack of self-control, she tried to wriggle out from beneath him but he was too strong.

'See, *cariño*,' he said, smothering her hands in his own and resting them on the table by her sides, his grip unyielding. 'The desire between us is as strong as it ever was, however much you try and deny it. When I ask you to open yourself for me, your head might want to say no but your body will be begging for it.'

That his words were true only served to shame her further, which she knew for certain was his intention. She'd humiliated him by leaving him and this was the price he was forcing her to pay.

The worst of it was, her treacherous body was eager to pay the price.

'I hate you.'

'I know.' He dipped his head and nipped her earlobe. 'Imagine how incredible it will be, all that hate fuelling all that lust.'

Sensation filled her, every crevice of her coming alive at his touch and the whisper of his breath on her skin.

Two years without this...

Somehow she managed to pull her hands free from his grasp, fully intending to use them as weapons to push him off her. Instead, working of their own accord, they hooked around his neck to pull him in for her hungry lips to connect with his. She had no sane comprehension of what she was doing, instinct taking over to seize what her body so desperately wanted.

In that instant, any sort of rationality dissolved from her mind.

In a mesh of lips and tongues, they came together, devouring each other, her fingers digging into his scalp, one of his hands sweeping up her back and nestling into her hair, clasping her head tightly.

His taste filled her, his warm breath merging with her own sending deeper darts of need into her, every part of her aching for his touch, his kiss, his caress...

The hand not cradling her head so possessively swept up her thigh and under her skirt, his mouth still hot on hers, his tongue swirling in her mouth. His finger found the band of her knickers and slid beneath it to feel the heat and dampness at the heart of her.

When he found her, already swollen and aching for him, she gasped...

And then he pulled away, releasing his hold so quickly her legs would have given way if the table hadn't been there to support her.

There was the tiniest moment when she caught Raul's own dazed incomprehension before his composure snapped back into place.

He smoothed his shirt down and nodded at the window. 'The gardener,' he said tightly.

A rumbling sound played in the distance and through the glass she caught a glimpse of a figure on a ride-on mower just metres from where they were...

It was enough to bring her to her senses.

What on earth had possessed her?

She tugged her skirt back down before straightening.

A taunting smile now played on his lips. 'See, *cariño*? I was right. All that hate fuels lust beautifully.'

She wiped her mouth defiantly, loathing herself for being the one to instigate the kiss as much as she loathed him for the mocking tone of his voice and his unscrupulous mind and the power he held over her.

'It won't happen again,' she promised through ragged breaths.

'I think you've told enough lies this past week, don't you?'

Raul sat back down and reached for a breadstick, waiting for the thunder beneath his ribcage to abate.

How had things got out of hand so quickly?

He'd been taunting her, teasing her, asserting his control, spelling out to her how much he held the upper hand. He'd enjoyed it but had kept his mind firmly on the seduction in hand.

She'd been the one to kiss him, a fact that, from the look on her face, she regretted hugely.

She'd hooked her arm around his neck and his mind had gone blank, desire overshadowing everything else.

The chemistry between them had always been explosive but that...

It had felt as if a coil locked in a too-tight box had finally sprung free.

He'd been seconds away from taking her on the table.

In his haste to free the house for them, he'd forgotten about the ground staff. If he hadn't heard the sound of the mower, who knew how far they would have taken it?

She still stood by the table, her green eyes firing their hatred at him.

Who did she hate the most? Him for compelling her back into his bed? Or herself for wanting it?

'So, *cariño*, do we have a deal?' He was gratified to hear his voice functioning as normal. He would *never* allow himself to show weakness in front of her. 'The day care centre, signed, sealed, delivered and renovated in exchange for four months in my bed?'

Four months. That would surely be enough to get her out of his system once and for all.

Maybe it was fortuitous that she'd walked back into his life at this moment. He needed to move on, not just from the dissolution of their marriage but from the sexual hold she still held over him.

Her chin rose, her pretty nostrils flaring. 'Yes. I accept your terms but with one condition of my own: I won't be sharing your bed until the deeds of the building are in my hands.'

'The building will be in the Cazorla name by the end of the week.'

'Then you'll have to wait until then before you can touch me again.'

'You are not in a position to make any demands, *cariño*.'

'Of course I am.' She swallowed but didn't waver. 'You can always go running back to your girlfriend if the frustration of waiting four days gets too much for you.'

'That relationship is over.' It hadn't even started.

Her lips curled into an expression that most closely resembled a sneer, but it was a fleeting look, quickly replaced by the loathing he was becoming familiar with.

Another four days?

He could force the issue if he wanted. It wouldn't be hard. All he had to do was touch her and she'd be putty in his hands.

Another four days?

The anticipation would be delicious.

He knew his wife and what an earthy, sexual creature she was. The chemistry between them was just as potent— if not more—as it had always been.

After four days of living together, Charley would be begging him to take her.

He'd managed almost two years. Another four days would be nothing.

'What time do you finish?' Raul asked when he pulled the car to a stop outside the building that currently housed the Poco Rio day care centre.

'Five o'clock,' she answered shortly. 'Wait for me to call—I might be late.'

'I'll be here at five o'clock and you will be ready.'

Not bothering to argue or say goodbye, she shrugged a shoulder, grabbed her bag and got out, slamming the passenger door behind her. She might not be able to see his face but could easily imagine her handsome husband's wince at her treatment of his precious Lotus.

When they'd first met, her manners had been somewhat rough around the edges. She'd been taught to say please and thank you, and not speak with her mouth full, but that had been the extent of it and those few manners had been drilled into her by her primary school headmistress, not her parents. Her mum had been too busy holding down two jobs to find the energy while her dad had hardly been there, flitting in and out of their lives as and when it suited him, which had never been enough, not for her.

She'd never lived with her father, had never spent a night under his roof and had lived for the days when he would visit his only daughter.

She remembered once begging her mum to move so they could be closer to him, remembered the anxiety on her mother's face at this impossibility. Her mum would do anything for her but to move the fifty miles would mean uprooting from the support network of her own loving and hardworking family.

Before they'd married, Raul had employed various people to 'help' Charley assimilate into Spanish high society. At the time it had felt as if she were starring in a rags-to-riches film and she'd been happy to embrace the elocution and deportment lessons, the drills on social niceties.

When she was growing up, meals at home had been spent beside her exhausted mum, with trays on their laps in front of the television, the pair of them happily arguing about whatever reality television programme they'd been into at that time. They'd hardly tasted the food. Their one proper meal of the week had come every Sunday when they would go to her grandparents' for a roast dinner, everyone squashed around the small kitchen table with huge mugs of tea in front of them.

Raul's world, with meals around a fully laid dining table with jugs of iced water, expensive wine, the savouring of food and the correct order of cutlery…it had been a different world. A fantastical dream come to life. Learning all these new things had been fun! At first.

It had taken a long time for her to realise that Raul had set out from the off to improve her so he could stand beside her without her being an embarrassment to the Cazorla name.

Their whole marriage had been about him moulding her into the sort of woman he believed she should be, the perfect wife he so desired.

She might have missed him terribly these past six hundred and thirty-six days but she had also been able to reclaim herself.

Leaving him had let her breathe again. She didn't have to introduce herself to people as Charlotte any more. She could simply be who she'd always been: Charley, the name Raul had never once addressed her by.

Whatever happened over these next four months, she

would not allow herself to lose sight of who she really was. Charley. Charlotte was merely the name on her birth certificate.

Inside the centre, she was greeted by Karin, a nine-year-old girl who'd been in a car crash as a baby. The crash had killed her father and left her with one functioning lung and severe brain damage. Yet, however locked in her own world Karin seemed, she always appeared to know when Charley was on the rota to work and would hang around the door of the day room until she arrived.

Charley scooped the skinny child up and planted a kiss on her cheek then gently set her back down and took her hand. Karin would be her shadow for the rest of the day, her easy affection something that warmed her heart.

A lump came to her throat as she looked at the dozen children in the day room, many locked in their own worlds, most of them here and alive against all the odds. *This* was what she was fighting for, these beautiful children. This was what she had to hold onto over the next four months.

For these children she would do anything. Even suffer living with her husband again.

CHAPTER FOUR

RAUL SAT IN his car scowling at his phone. It was almost five-thirty and Charley hadn't yet come out. Nor was she answering his calls.

He looked at the building again, debating for the tenth time whether or not to go inside and get her. To his eyes the place looked like nothing but a load of concrete blocks slapped together. The only spot of colour was a faded sign above the door that read Poco Rio. Little River. The name would have amused him—for a start, the Turia had run nowhere near this part of Valencia even before the devastating floods of 1957, which had caused the authorities to divert it to skirt the city rather than run through it—but instead he shuddered. Who would want their child to spend their days in a place like this? Far from the sunny exterior most day care centres projected, this building, with its drab grounds…everything about it shouted 'institution'.

His mind flickered to the care home his father had spent time in after his stroke while his mother had turned a wing of the family home into a facility able to manage his twenty-four-hour needs. That care home had been more akin to a hotel, a beautiful villa set in luscious grounds with first-class staff.

The care home could have been as opulent as the very first Cazorla hotel, built by Raul's grandfather, Nestor Cazorla, in 1955, and Eduardo Cazorla would still have hated it, even if he couldn't vocalise his thoughts or feelings. That hotel, built in Madrid, had been a shot in the eye to the Ritzes and Waldorfs of this world, a statement that anything they could do, the Cazorlas could do too.

Under Eduardo's reign, the Cazorla Hotel Madrid fell from its lofty heights, as did the other thirty-eight hotels in the chain. Investment became a dirty word, Eduardo preferring to spend the dwindling profits on maintaining his lifestyle.

Raul clearly remembered the day when he'd sat down with his father to discuss the shocking decline of the family business. He'd graduated from university with a mile-long list of ideas for improvement. He'd mistakenly thought that gaining a first-class degree from MIT would finally garner his father's respect. If not respect then at least something more than the distaste that seemed to be his father's default emotion towards him.

His father had calmly sat at his desk and flipped through the pages and pages of analysis and reports Raul had completed, then, still calm, had walked to his office window, opened it, and thrown the pages out onto the street below.

Then he'd turned back to his son and said, 'That's what I think of your ideas.'

After twenty-two years of Raul's being on the receiving end of his father's relentless criticism, something inside him had snapped. He'd walked out of his father's office without a word, returned to the family home, packed his bags, and left, using the small cash inheritance he'd received when Nestor died to rent an apartment and invest in a friend's fledgling technology business. He'd recouped his investment in three months and immediately set out to invest in another.

He'd spent his entire life striving to be the perfect son his father wanted; now he was going to be the man *he* wanted to be. What he wanted above all else was to be *nothing* like his father.

As his business had grown, not once had his father asked any questions about it. Raul had no idea whether he had been pleased or disappointed that his only son had bailed on the family firm. When they had been together as a family no one had spoken of or alluded to it; not even his mother, who came from a wealthy, high-society family in her own right. So long as Raul had still played at being the dutiful son, kept the perfect Cazorla face intact, joined them at important family functions and kept the family name away from the scandal rags that had been good enough for her.

He was pulled out of his reminiscences when a dark blue minibus drove into the grounds and pulled up beside him. He paid little attention to it until he caught the figure getting out of the driver's side.

While he was processing the image of Charley driving a minibus, she spotted him and, unsmiling, held up a hand and mouthed, 'Five minutes.'

He shoved his door open. 'We need to leave now. You're late enough as it is.'

'I did warn you,' she replied with a nonchalant shrug. 'I need to drop the keys back in and sign off. I won't be long.'

She hurried off in her jeans-clad legs and disappeared through the double front door.

He could still hardly believe his wife was wearing jeans. He didn't think he'd ever seen her in a pair before.

When he'd refused to take her back to her house in Valencia the night before, although promising to get her to work on time that morning, she hadn't argued. He'd been quietly satisfied that she was adapting to his authority well, right until he'd discovered her missing. She'd returned a couple of hours later with a bag of shopping, saying, 'You can hardly expect me to go to work wearing Chanel.' Thus she had proceeded to take herself off to one of the spare rooms she'd appropriated for her own use, locked the door, and refused to come out until the morning.

He'd been sorely tempted to kick said door down but had refrained from losing his cool in any fashion. He'd left her alone, dining on marinated fillet of pork while she stayed hungry, stewing in her own righteousness.

Come Friday she would be in his bedroom with him. If she refused, she knew what the consequences would be. No more funds for her pet project.

When she reappeared exactly five minutes later, she got into the car and slammed the door.

'You're doing that deliberately, aren't you?' he said through gritted teeth.

'Sorry.'

She didn't sound in the least bit sorry.

Grinding his teeth some more, he reversed, turned round and drove out of the car park.

'Why were you driving that thing anyway?'

'I was taking some of the kids home.'

Now he recalled her mention of her car the day before. 'When did you pass your driving test?'

'A year ago.'

'I always said there was nothing to be frightened of and that you were capable of driving over here.' She'd learned to drive in England but had never taken a test. Despite all his cajoling and his offer to buy her any car she desired, she'd always flatly refused to get behind the wheel of a car in Spain.

It felt like a slap to know she'd waited until she was out of his life before trying for her licence.

'You're always right,' Charley said shortly, thinking of all the times she'd heard the words 'I told you' from his lips, before quickly adding, 'I needed to be able to drive for the job. We take it in turns to collect the kids and drop them back, at least for the ones whose parents don't drive.'

Looking back, she couldn't believe it had taken her so long to take her test. She'd been even more surprised when she'd passed first time. She'd been *convinced* she was going to fail.

When the examiner had told her she'd passed, her first impulse had been to call Raul and share the news with him. Finally she'd passed something—it had been a heady moment.

'I assume you charge extra for the taxiing service?' he said.

She shot him a look. 'Of course we don't.'

'That's something that will have to change. You're throwing money away.'

Charley breathed deeply, biting back every nasty name she wanted to throw at him.

She'd always known her husband was materialistic but this was something else. How could he have such an attitude towards those poor children?

'Do you know where I live?' she asked, deliberately changing the subject before she gave in to the urge to punch him.

'Your address was on the divorce papers.'

They lapsed into silence for the rest of the short journey to her home.

'*This* is your house?' Raul asked when he pulled into her driveway.

'Not what you were expecting?'

'I was expecting something more lavish.' His lips formed a mocking smile. 'What happened? Did you have to sell up when the money started to run out?'

She kept her gaze on him even. 'I bought this house six

months after I left you. Lavish is your style, not mine.' Her two-bedroom villa was modest but more than adequate for her needs. It might not have its own swimming pool or a beach at the bottom of the garden but nor did it have so many rooms she needed a map to find her way around.

'That's not how I remember things.'

Oh, yes. That was right. He thought she was a gold-digger. 'I don't control your memories.'

'And neither do you control your finances.'

Fighting the rising anger, Charley tugged at her bag and rummaged through for her keys. 'Let's get this done.'

Inside, she headed straight to her bedroom and began to pack, carefully placing her clothes into the same Louis Vuitton suitcases she'd used when she'd left him. She could hear Raul giving himself a tour of her home. It was a very short tour. Minutes later he was in her room watching her put the last of her stuff into the cases.

'Are you nearly done?'

'Yes. Whatever we can't fit in the car today I'll collect on Friday.' On Friday they would be coming back to Valencia. She would work at the centre while Raul finalised the purchase of the new building. As far as Raul was concerned, her shift at the centre would be her last. She wasn't prepared to argue about it until the deeds were signed and in her hands.

Raul heaved her cases off the bed and carried them to the car. Charley slipped into the spare room she used as an office and gathered all her plans together.

'What's that?' he asked, entering the tiny space a short while later, standing behind her and immediately making it feel even more cramped than usual.

'The plans for the redevelopment of the new centre.'

'Don't bother with them,' he said dismissively. 'I'll get my own architect onto it.'

She placed everything into the briefcase she'd taken to the bank manager only the day before, sliding it on top of the financial aspects of the loan she had pored over for hours. *Do not bite,* she warned herself. *Raul still has a number of days to change his mind. Do not bite.* 'Your architect can use these plans to guide him.'

'You think you know better than an architect with twenty years' experience?'

'I think this is something to be discussed when the deeds have been signed.' *Until then, do not bite.*

'*Cariño*, do not forget, this project is now under my control.' He stepped closer to her, close enough that she could feel his heat warm her back. His voice dropped to a murmur. She could feel his breath in her hair. 'As are you.'

Charley froze, keeping herself ramrod straight, and swallowed the moisture that filled her mouth.

How did he *do* this? How did he make her want him so much while simultaneously making her want to scratch her nails down his face?

'I'm not yours until Friday,' she reminded him in a strangled voice. 'No touching until then.'

'I don't think you'll make me wait that long.'

'I hate you.'

'I know.' His breath whispered through the strands of her hair, heating her scalp. 'It must be awful for you, hating me so much but wanting me even more.'

'I don't want you.'

'I never realised when we married what a liar you are.' The tip of his nose nestled into her hair. 'If I hadn't been so blinded by lust I would have known your words of love and your promise of a child were nothing but lies to access my fortune.'

His tone was playful but when Charley spun round to face him she saw the darkness in his eyes.

'I didn't lie to you and I didn't marry you for your money.' She *hated* that he thought of her as a gold-digger, making out that the times when they'd been happy together—and there had been times when she'd been delirious with happiness—were nothing but a lie.

'Then what did you marry me for? My wit and personality?' he taunted in that same playful way, as the darkness in his eyes turned cold.

'You.' She felt heat creep up her neck. 'I married you for *you*. I thought you were wonderful.'

He feigned injury. 'You don't think I'm wonderful any more?'

'I think you're cruel. You're using those poor children as pawns to get me back into your bed and all because of some ridiculous notion of revenge because I wouldn't have your baby.'

Where her words came from she didn't know and she would gladly have swallowed them back if she could, but they spurted out as if they had a force of their own.

His eyes had gone cold enough to make her shiver. But the smile hadn't dropped. He leaned forward and brushed his cheek to hers. 'It's not revenge, *cariño*. I'm giving you what you want. In return you're giving me what I want.'

'My body.'

'Exactly that.' He nuzzled against her cheek. 'But if it *was* revenge I sought, then having you back in my bed would be the sweetest-tasting revenge there is.'

'I think you're cruel.'

That was what Charley had said.

Was he being cruel?

Raul didn't like to think of himself as cruel. His own father, when he'd been in good health, had had a great capacity for cruelty and it was a trait Raul had sworn he would never adopt. He was prepared to accept that he was forceful and direct, arrogant even, but never cruel. Not until the woman he'd lavished everything on thought she could come to him for help as if nothing had passed between them.

He forced his mind back to their marriage. He'd been happy to indulge her when she'd announced she wanted to run a luxury chauffeur hire for travelling business people. He'd had his doubts from the off—for a start, Charley couldn't drive, but, as she'd pointed out, she would employ drivers. Despite his misgivings, he'd given her the money to buy a handful of limousines and premises from which to run the business. With his extensive contacts book at her disposal, he'd seen no reason why her fledgling business should be anything other than a success.

A year later, the company had folded. Contracts had dried up and instead of coming to him for help she had thrown in the towel.

He'd tried to be understanding. It was a big thing she'd undertaken, starting a business of her own, especially coming into it with no qualifications or business experience.

The next venture she'd embarked on, he'd supplied her with both his financial backing and a team of his personal staff to help her with it all. It had gone bust within four months. The third—which he couldn't even remember—had lasted only a month longer.

It was after that third and final venture that he'd sat her down and insisted it was time for her to stop playing at business and time for them to start the family she'd promised him.

His stomach soured as he recalled her reaction. It was as if he'd thrown a pot of boiling water over her.

He took a breath and pushed her bedroom door open.

She was in the adjoining room, sitting at the large desk below the window, papers spread out before her.

'We need to leave in an hour.' He'd informed her over breakfast that morning that they would be dining out with friends that evening.

She didn't look at him. 'I'll be ready.'

'Charlotte, it takes you at least two hours to get ready for a night out.' And that was if he was lucky. She had a tendency to try on her entire wardrobe before deciding on an outfit, then she would tease her hair into a dozen different styles before deciding which was the 'right' one. It didn't matter how many times he told her, she never seemed to believe him when he said she was beautiful in whatever she wore.

A sudden memory brushed through him, of their honeymoon, where he'd flown her to a private island in the Caribbean. It had been the last time he'd truly seen her full of spirit and abandon. One night, when he'd been gently chivvying her to get ready for dinner, she'd stripped her clothes off with glee and charged off to the private cove the island's staff were banned from, splashing naked in the water with such joy it had compelled him to strip off his own clothes and join her, and make love to her.

His chest filled as he recalled how special that moment had been, the freedom he'd felt with the sun bathing down on his naked form and his wife's supple limbs wrapped around him.

Of all the good moments within their marriage, this was the memory that stood out for him, the vivid remembrance of the belief that they were the happiest, most perfect couple in the world.

'I'll be ready,' she repeated.

'What are you doing?'

'Going over the plans for the development.'

'What for? I told you, I'll be using my own team.'

Her shoulders raised stubbornly. 'I've put hundreds of hours into this. It's stupid not to at least take it into account.'

'I'm sure my architect will be delighted to have your input,' he drawled.

Shoving her chair back, she got to her feet. 'I'm going to take a shower,' she said, her voice tight.

'One hour.'

'So you keep telling me.' She closed the adjoining door firmly behind her. He heard the lock slide into place.

Raul flexed his fingers and took a deep breath.

The past four days had been like living with a sullen teenager. He'd given her a little leeway, which had been decent of him under the circumstances, but from now on he would not put up with it.

Tomorrow, the deeds would be signed and she would be indebted to him.

Curiosity made him look at the papers sprawled over her desk.

A few moments later he sat on the chair still warm from her body heat with a frown on his face.

Peering more closely through the stack before him, he saw she'd taken each room of the new building and committed to paper her ideas for the renovations. Each drawing was done to scale.

Charley had said she'd done these plans.

Had she been lying in an attempt to impress him?

But no—the notes in the margins, the numbers indicating the measurements, these were all in her girlish writing.

He rubbed at his temples, his chest tightening as he imagined her sitting in that tiny study in the tiny home she'd been living in, working diligently on these plans. Alone.

* * *

After a quick shower and shave, Raul found Charley in the living room.

'You're ready?' he asked, astonished to find her waiting for him. He was equally astounded at what she was wearing: a pair of cropped grey figure-hugging patchwork trousers and a sheer black blouse. On her feet were a pair of flat black strappy sandals.

'Yes.' Rising from the sofa, she passed the window, the low early evening sun shining through to allow him to see perfectly the lacy black bra she wore beneath the seemingly modest blouse.

'What?' she asked, a scowl forming.

'Are you really intending to go out for a meal with friends wearing that?'

'Yes, Raul, I am. Why? Is there something wrong with it?'

'I'm surprised, that's all.' She looked good—she looked beautiful—there was no denying that but he could not recall a single time after they'd married when she'd worn trousers or jeans. Now, other than the party she'd gate-crashed and the morning of her meeting with the bank manager, he'd not seen a single sign of her legs. The Charley he'd been married to wouldn't have dreamed of going out for dinner in anything less than a designer dress and five-inch heels. She would hardly *breakfast* in anything less.

'This is what I have in my wardrobe.'

'What happened to the rest of your clothes?' Charley had had a wall at the back of her walk-in wardrobe filled with shoes alone. Thinking about it, he couldn't see how her tiny Valencian bedroom would fit even a fraction of her clothes in it.

'I gave most of them to charity shops.'

'What did you do that for?'

She shrugged. 'There's not much call for Dolce & Gabbana at Poco Rio.'

'I'll give my sister a ring and see if she's free to go on a shopping trip with you over the next few days.' He reached into his pocket for his phone.

Charley folded her arms and shook her head, but the scowl disappeared, replaced by a look that was almost... sad. 'I don't want to go on a shopping trip. I like my wardrobe just fine as it is.'

'Charlotte,' he said, striving for patience, 'over the next four months we will be dining out and socialising as we always used to do. The clothes you have are fine for what you've been doing at the centre but those days are currently over. You're my wife and you know what that means.'

'That I have to dress up like a doll?'

'No.' She was being deliberately obtuse. 'But being a Cazorla does mean projecting a certain image—'

'Why?'

He rubbed the nape of his neck and whistled air through his teeth. 'We discussed this when we first became engaged. My family is highly respected here, our hotels some of the finest in the world. People look up to us.'

It had been for her sake that he'd wanted her to fit in. He knew what it was like to be judged as not good enough and had never wanted that for her. He hadn't wanted the woman he loved to enter a social situation and feel insecure about *anything*. He'd done his best to give her all the tools she'd needed to assimilate into high society as if she'd been born into it.

'I still don't understand why that means I have to dress like a doll.'

'You don't have to "dress like a doll",' he said, his jaws clamping together. 'I really don't understand what the problem is. You loved dressing up when we lived together before.'

He remembered the light in her eyes after that first shopping trip with Marta and their personal shopper and Charley's bursts of laughter as she'd carefully taken each item out of its box for him to look at and comment on. Her happiness hadn't been fake, of that he was certain.

The corners of her lips curved into a whimsical smile, the closest thing to a real smile he'd seen all week, although there was nothing happy about it.

'I did at first, yes. But what twenty-year-old *wouldn't* love being let loose in one of the most exclusive shopping arcades in Europe with an unlimited credit card?'

'So you admit, you *did* marry me for my money?'

She shook her head, her blonde hair brushing over her shoulders. 'I won't lie; your wealth turned my head. Your whole lifestyle did. But I would have married you if you'd lived in a shack.'

He laughed humourlessly. 'It is lucky your nose is not like Pinocchio's or it would be sprouting leaves as we speak.'

Her eyes held his. 'If I'm such a gold-digger, why did I walk away and leave it all behind?'

'You left with ten million euros.'

'Money I never asked for,' she pointed out. 'And you know as well as I do I could have asked for a whole lot more.'

'And you know as well as I do that until our divorce is final, you still can.' He reached out a hand and traced a finger down her cheek, not liking the disquiet prodding at him.

She was right. She *hadn't* asked for his money. He'd given it freely.

Nor had she asked for the credit cards and everything

else he'd given her when he'd wanted nothing more than to see that smile from her first shopping trip replicated.

None of that mattered any more. The only smile he wanted to see on her face now was the smile of pleasure.

One more night of sleeping on his own and she would be his again.

'It is hardly coincidence that you returned to my life when the money had almost run out,' he pointed out.

She made to speak but he cut her off by rubbing his thumb over her lips. 'If you play your cards right over the next four months, you will find my generosity knows no limits. Play your cards right and I will give you so much money it would take you a lifetime to spend it.'

She slapped his hand away, angry colour heightening her cheeks. 'Once the centre has been redeveloped, the only thing I will want from you is my freedom.'

'Your freedom will be guaranteed.' Unable to resist dropping his face into her neck and inhaling that musky vanilla scent that turned him on so much, he added, 'And so will mine.'

CHAPTER FIVE

CHARLEY WAS OUT of the centre before Raul's watch registered her being even one minute late. She hurried to the car, her excitement tangible. She'd been the same that morning, unable to keep still for a second, downing coffee as if it were going out of fashion but unable to eat a morsel of the eggs his chef had cooked for them.

She pulled the passenger door open. 'Is it done?'

'Yes.'

She punched the air. 'Thank God.'

'You're welcome. But Raul will suffice.'

She pulled a face at him and laughed. 'Right now, I'm so happy and grateful I'll call you anything you like.'

He bit back the quip forming on his tongue, not wanting to break the moment. Seeing the delight on her face lightened his blood.

It had been a long time since he'd seen that smile.

A skinny, balding man poked his head out of the building. Abandoning Raul, Charley hurried over to him, hurled her arms around his waist and kissed his cheek. The man disappeared back inside with a beaming grin of his own.

She rushed back to the car, jumped in, shut the door without slamming it and yanked out the band holding her hair in a ponytail. Tidying her hair with her fingers, she looked at him, her eyes bright with excitement.

'Who was that?' he asked in as nonchalant a voice as he

could muster. Watching his wife throw her arms around another man had felt...disturbing, like having pins stuck into his flesh.

For the first time, he confronted the possibility that there had been another man in her life since they'd parted.

Two years was a long time to be alone.

'Seve—he runs the centre. He'll be sharing the good news with the others.' Charley's happiness was so infectious even the car seemed to react to it, an upbeat song playing out from the radio.

But what was she so happy about? Raul's purchase of the building? Or the fact she'd spent most of the day with *Seve*?

'I hope they enjoy the moment.' He killed the radio and put the car into gear. It was only three p.m.; if traffic was kind, they could be back in Barcelona within a couple of hours. His helicopter pilot was primed for take-off.

'I'm sure they'll celebrate all night.'

'Do you wish you were celebrating with them?'

'I would *love* to.' The longing was clear in her voice.

If she was hoping he'd relent and let her stay in Valencia for the night, she was doomed to disappointment. They'd made a deal. From this moment on, Charley was *his*.

'This Seve, he is a good friend of yours?'

'Yes.'

'Is that all he is to you? A friend?'

She twisted in her seat to stare at him. 'Are you trying to find out if Seve and I are lovers?'

'Are you?'

'He's married.'

'And so are *you*.'

Her cheeks tightened. 'I wouldn't be if you'd signed the divorce papers when you'd first got them, but even if I wasn't, I wouldn't mess about with a married man.'

'And what about single men? Have you "messed about" with many of them since you left?'

She was silent for a moment before answering, her voice as taut as her features. 'I will tell you how many men I've messed around with after you tell me how many women you've been with. Obviously I know about Jessica, so that's one. How many others?'

If she only knew the truth.

How would she react if he were to tell her that since she'd left there hadn't been anyone else? He would visit his hotels and cruise liners, be surrounded by semi-naked women flirting outrageously with him, and feel nothing. He might as well have been dead from the waist down. Jessica was famed as one of the sexiest women in the world but even she'd left him cold.

He wouldn't give Charley the satisfaction of the truth.

But neither did he want to hear if she'd had other lovers in their time apart. Nothing good could come of it.

Four months was ample time to get her out of his system. By the time those months were over, his libido would surely be begging for variety.

'Giving numbers is vulgar and unbecoming,' he said smoothly.

'I quite agree.'

His gaze darted briefly to her. 'But to be clear, while you are back in my bed, there will be no other men in your life.'

'I'm only yours until the renovations are complete,' she reminded him with a pointed look. All the euphoria she'd displayed when she'd got into the car had now gone.

'But until then, *cariño*, you are *mine*.' To reiterate his point, he put a hand on her thigh and squeezed it lightly, before moving it to change gear.

He heard her suck in a breath and hold it for the longest time.

'Have you got the deeds?' she asked, her voice now flat.

'I have a copy of them in my briefcase. You can have them when we get home.'

Soon enough they would be back.

Soon enough she would be back in his bed, right where she belonged.

If she'd had any lovers in the time they'd been apart he would ensure they were obliterated from her memory, leaving only him.

Yes. Tonight she would be his again. All his.

Charley entered the villa feeling as if the weight of the world had landed back on her shoulders.

For a few brief minutes, when Raul had confirmed the purchase of the new building, she'd felt so light-headed she wouldn't have needed the helicopter to fly.

Then he'd ruined it all by implying there was something romantic going on between her and Seve. This, from the man who'd been bedding a hot lingerie model.

Raul had carried on with his life as if she'd never been a part of it. All her paranoia from their marriage had come true, her secret fear that, as had always been the case with her father, when Charley was out of someone's sight she was out of their mind. Forgettable. Replaceable.

Raul had moved on. New home, new lover, new everything.

If only it had been as easy for her to move on too.

Her life had become rich with friends—real friends; their meal with Diego and Elana the previous night had brought home to her how wonderful it was to *have* true friends. Elana's friendship had been foisted upon her when she and Raul had first got together. Originally a receptionist for Diego's world-famous plastic-surgery practice, Elana was now the epitome of high-society goddess with a perfectly straight nose, sculpted cheekbones and inflated breasts. All of the other 'friends' Charley had made in their time together had been of an identical mould.

Far too well-mannered to say anything derogatory about Charley's outfit, Elana had been unable to hide the flicker of shock when she'd cast her eyes over her. For her part, Elana had been dressed from top to tail in the required designer label, her gold shoes so high Charley had felt sorry for her feet. Not even the red stilettos she'd forced her feet into on Saturday night had been that high.

Looking back, Charley struggled to understand how she'd allowed herself to suffer such self-inflicted torture. She'd thought nothing of wearing five-inch heels for a full day at work.

But it had been expected of her. She had been the wife of Raul Cazorla and she had been expected to dress and act the part, including cultivating friendships with like-minded women.

The only real friendship she'd made had been, funnily enough, with Marta, Raul's sister, who was an incredibly smart and amusing woman.

The strange thing was, while they'd been eating last night, she'd noticed so many new things: the way Elana picked at her food as if scared to consume a calorie more than was good for her, the way she deferred to her husband before offering an opinion...all the things Charley had once done. And just like that, she'd seen all the insecurities running under Elana's surgically lifted skin. Being the trophy wife of a successful, rich, handsome man wasn't all it was cracked up to be. Charley should know. It had broken her in the end.

Even so, there was no hiding away from the knowledge that for the past two years she'd been empty inside, as if a big hollow had opened up in her belly. She hadn't so much as looked at another man.

Raul called out to her from the living area.

She found him pouring a bottle of red into two glasses. He handed one to her.

'To us,' he said, raising his glass.

'To the new centre,' she corrected, chinking her glass against his.

'You can't have one without the other.' His eyes gleamed. 'I have given you what you want. Now it is time for you to fulfil your end of the bargain.'

It didn't take Einstein to know what he meant, or a mind-reader to read his thoughts.

He took a sip of wine, his full lips pressing together as he swallowed, his blue eyes holding hers in the way that had always made her melt.

She did the same now, a rush of heat pooling low in her belly and spreading out to her limbs.

Her mind ran amok as she took a steadying sip of her own wine, remembering all the nights they'd come together, devouring each other, loving each other...

Don't go there, Charley. He never loved you, only loved who he wanted you to be. You were never good enough for him as you were. You're worth even less now, nothing more than a warm body for him to use to sate himself whenever and wherever the mood strikes.

She was good for only one thing. He'd spelled that out loud and clear. And now he wanted his payment.

It was the reminder she needed.

The reality of making love—no, *having sex*—with him for the first time in such a manner had the effect of making her libido nosedive to her toes.

Whatever wrongs he might believe she'd done to him, she deserved more than to be taken at his command and only for his pleasure. Whatever gratitude she might feel for him saving the centre plummeted with her libido. The financial cost to Raul was so tiny in comparison to his wealth it would be akin to a normal person buying a bottle of wine.

She cleared her throat, determined to stall the moment for as long as she could. 'I would like to take a look at the deeds.'

The strangest expression came into his eyes. 'As you wish.'

He stepped over to his briefcase, which he'd placed on the bureau, and unlocked it. About to open it, he was distracted by his phone vibrating. He grimaced and shrugged before pulling it out of his pocket, looking at the screen, and deciding whoever was on the other end was worthy of his attention.

He left the living room and disappeared, she assumed to his study.

Relieved for a few more minutes' grace, she pulled her own phone out of her bag and answered the dozens of messages that had come through from overjoyed staff and the children's parents alike, all of whom had been waiting on tenterhooks like her.

Done, she stared at Raul's briefcase, which was still where he'd left it, unlocked.

Unable to wait a moment longer, she opened it and pulled out a hefty brown envelope lying on the top. She had a quick peek to make sure it was the deeds and not another business-related document that was none of her concern.

A fresh wave of excitement swept through her when she saw the address of the new centre in the middle of the cover page. She pulled the thick sheath of papers out of the envelope and rifled through them, her mind awhirl with all the plans she had for the centre, plans that would now become a reality.

Her grasp of Spanish had increased greatly in the past two years but legalese was a whole new ballpark. All the same, she persevered, right through to the last page. By then she'd finished her wine and was ready for another glass, but, rather than pour herself one, she stared at the pages with a frown.

Something bugged her. She couldn't think what it could be but her intuition told her something was off.

She started scanning the pages again, fiddling with a lock of hair as she forced herself to concentrate...

The bastard!

Now she knew what was wrong.

Sucking on her little finger, she skimmed through all the papers one more time looking in vain for her name.

In a maelstrom of anger and indignation, she stormed to his office and shoved the door open.

Raul was sitting at his desk, phone in one hand, a pen twirling between the fingers of his other.

'You lying, manipulative...' she said, throwing the deeds onto his desk.

He stilled for a moment, then spoke quietly into the phone and disconnected the call.

'Has something upset you?' he asked with steely calm.

'These deeds are in your name.'

'Yes,' he agreed.

'You said the building would be mine.'

'No, I said the building would be in the Cazorla name and that is exactly what I have done.'

'You know perfectly well I thought it was being put in my name. I was going to form a trust and hand it over to the centre!'

He laughed. 'Then it seems I made a wise decision to

put it in *my* name. What do a bunch of childminders know about managing a project such as this?'

'Don't speak so...so derogatorily about them,' she snarled, pulling the word out after having it trip over her tongue. She hadn't even known what derogatory meant five years ago. 'Besides, they weren't going to manage the project, *I* was, and I know a lot more than you credit me for. I didn't go into this lightly.'

'Maybe you did, maybe you didn't; it doesn't change the fact that you couldn't get the financing for it and for the very good reason that your track record in business is abysmal.'

'You're *sick*,' she seethed. 'You've done this deliberately, haven't you?'

He shrugged. 'Does it matter? The end effect is the same—the building will be used for a new centre.'

'But under your control.'

'I am not a team player, *cariño*. I don't deal with collaboration. You will get your centre but you will not have the opportunity to mess up the renovations.'

'I am not going to mess this up!' she shouted.

He gave her a measured stare. 'Control your temper. It is most unattractive.'

'Do you think I care what *you* find attractive?'

'You should, considering the project hasn't even started yet.'

She knew exactly what he meant. 'Are you seriously serious? If I don't toe the line then you'll pull the plug?'

'If necessary. But as I've said numerous times, if you fulfil your side of the bargain then I will fulfil mine.'

'You *lied* to me.'

'No. You made assumptions.' He rose from his seat and rested his hand on the desk, leaning forward. 'I made it very clear that I would be taking control. I will be in charge and you will be by my side. Look at it from a positive perspective—this time you'll see how a project is conducted properly all the way to its conclusion.'

The anger inside her had risen so high it threatened to choke her. The worst of it was that she knew he was right. She *had* made assumptions.

But, damn him, he'd let her.

She'd known from the start that her husband was a competitive man who had to be the best at everything he did. He wasn't satisfied until he'd mastered whatever he'd set out to do. In this case he'd set out to master *her*, to punish her for her refusal to have the child he thought was his due.

Unable to be in the same room as him for a moment longer lest she throw something at him, she stormed out and ran up the stairs to the sanctuary of the room she'd made her own.

The room was empty.

She checked the wardrobe, the dresser and the bathroom. Every single one of her possessions had gone. The bed had been stripped, the white mattress and plump pillows lying there uncovered as if in forlorn sympathy for her.

'Your belongings have been moved into my bedroom.'

She spun around to find Raul pressed against the doorway.

'Nice to know you didn't waste any time,' she said, not bothering to hide her contempt.

He smiled lazily and stepped over to her, placing his hands on the tops of her arms and leaning down to breathe into her hair. 'Your anger is a waste of your energy.' His voice dropped as he slid his hands down her sleeved arms and covered her balled fists. 'Come, let me show you where you'll be sleeping for the next four months.'

'I'd rather sleep in a box,' she hissed, somehow managing to hold back the burn of angry tears that had welled in her eyes.

'*Cariño*, are you deliberately trying to rouse my anger?' he asked in a caressing tone that contained an edge of warning.

'Why should I be the only one to be angry?' she demanded. 'You've hoodwinked me.'

'I'm investing a great deal of money in your scheme and I want to protect it.'

She forced her voice to remain calm. 'Will you sign the deeds over to me when the renovations are complete?'

He contemplated her silently and his blue eyes narrowed. '*If* you can prove yourself to be focused, and by that I mean that you *keep* your focus until the renovations are complete, then I might consider signing it over to you.'

'Might?'

'I will not make a false promise, *cariño*.' His voice dropped to a purr and he dipped his face into the curve of her neck and traced his lips gently over her skin. 'Enough talk about deeds and renovations. I can think of a much better way to pass the time.'

She dug her still-too-short nails into her palms, far too aware of his warm fingers holding her, his hot breath sensitising her skin... How *could* she still want him?

Something hot flickered in her belly, a resolve that pushed through her fury, taming it enough so she loosened her fists and laced her fingers through his.

So he wanted her, did he? Well, let him have her.

CHAPTER SIX

WITH CHARLEY'S FINGERS linked through his, Raul led her out of the empty room, down the wide landing and up a set of narrow wooden stairs to the top floor.

As soon as they stepped over the threshold into his bedroom she dropped his hand, kicked her sandals off then marched over to stand in the centre of the room.

Her eyes fixed on his, she tugged her top up and off.

No sooner had her top hit the floor than she was undoing the buttons of her shorts and letting them drop to her feet, where she stepped out of them and kicked them away.

He stood, transfixed at the scenario playing out before him, his eyes drinking in the unexpected striptease his wife was performing for him.

Her green eyes flashing, she unclasped her white bra, which went the same way as the rest of her clothes, then pinched the sides of her matching knickers, skimming them down her hips from where gravity took care of the rest.

When all her clothes were lying in a pool beside her, she put her hands on her hips and jutted out her chin.

He made to step towards her but something held him back.

Her eyes burned, but it wasn't with desire. It was with defiance. Her whole body vibrated with it.

'Well?' she said, the challenge in her voice clear. 'I'm here. I'm ready. I'm willing. If you want me, then *take* me.'

Her figure was exquisite, with her full breasts and succulent nipples, the feminine swell of her abdomen and the rounded hips that topped long, shapely legs. At the juncture of her thighs lay the soft dark brown curls he'd once loved running his fingers over.

He remembered the first time he'd seen her naked. At the time she'd been platinum blonde. He'd laughed when he'd pulled her knickers off and seen the dark hair there, the only evidence of her natural colouring. He'd especially liked kissing her there, that first time and all the others, feeling her excitement mount as she'd press upwards and into him, her gasps of pleasure seeping through his skin.

Memories flooded him, vivid and colourful. His wife had always been putty in his hands. It would be so easy to kiss all that defiance away. The sweetest, easiest thing in the world.

The heat running through his loins had turned the ache inside him into a form of pain.

He ignored it.

Folding his arms, he shook his head and clicked his tongue against the roof of his mouth.

She trembled as he walked to her but her chin didn't drop, not even when he reached an arm round to cup her bottom.

'You want me to take you now, do you?' he whispered, pulling her flush against him, tracing his fingers up her bare back, then gathering her thick mop of hair together and spearing his fingers through it.

'You can do whatever you like,' she whispered back, her breaths coming in shallow hitches.

But when his lips met hers, he found her mouth unyielding.

'You said I could do whatever I like.'

'And you can. But that doesn't mean I have to partici-
pate or enjoy it.'

He tugged her hair back and stared into her insolent
eyes. Anger flooded through him at the confirmation of
the game she was playing. But he tempered it.

She wanted to play?

Nothing would give him greater pleasure.

And she would learn that whatever game she played
with him, she would never win.

He released his hold on her and swept his fingers over
her shoulders, down over her breasts, lightly pinching those
gorgeous nipples, already hard with the arousal she wished
to deny, in the way that had always made her moan.

There were no moans this time, but her lips parted a
fraction, her cheeks heightening with colour. The defiance remained.

'Sit on the chair,' he commanded, indicating the arm-
chair in the corner of the room.

'What?'

'Sit on the chair. You said I could do whatever I like,
and what I would like is for you to sit on that chair.'

She swallowed, looking at the chair as if it might be
a trap.

'I can carry you if you'd prefer?'

Her eyes dilated at his words but her chin rose. She
turned and walked to it, her back straight and her head
high, goddess-like.

When she sat down, her eyes met his. *You can make
me do anything you like but you won't make me enjoy it*,
they said.

Smiling, he stalked towards her and dropped to his
knees. Without a word, he gripped her thighs and pulled
her towards him so that his face was level with the place

he so desperately wanted to taste. Just the thought of it made him want to plunge deep inside her.

Instead, he mustered all his discipline and spread her thighs, waiting, teasing.

She didn't move, her body rigid.

Whatever fight was occurring between Charley's mind and body, her body was winning. He rubbed his thumb along the delicate folds, his eyes gleaming as he found her hot and moist. When his tongue finally found her, he gave a growl of appreciation.

Her body remained unyielding, right until he found the rhythm he knew she loved. The tiniest of moans escaped from her.

Keeping the pressure light but firm, his hands stroking the soft skin of her thighs and stomach, slowly but surely he felt her relax into his ministrations.

He felt fit to burst himself, especially when her hands finally gripped his head, her fingers scraping at his scalp. She raised her hips to increase the pressure. Only by the skin of his teeth did he keep himself in check, intent only on her pleasure. Her moans deepened breath by breath until her body went rigid all over again...but this time in ecstasy.

He kept his mouth and tongue exactly where they were, absorbing the shudders that racked through her right until she dropped her hold on him and lay back.

His heart thumping painfully, Raul raised his head to look at her.

She was staring at the ceiling, her chest rising and falling as if she were struggling to get air into her lungs.

Not until he got to his feet did she deign to look at him. Her eyes were wide and dazed but he could see the defiance creeping back into them.

How easy it would be to take off his trousers and free

himself, to enter her, to obliterate the rising insolence in her eyes and bring her to a second climax.

But that would be to let her win.

In this game of desire there would only be one winner.

When she opened her legs for him, he wanted her screaming his name not fighting it, and if he had to suffer to achieve that aim then so be it. He was a big boy. He would cope.

'I'm going to take a shower. Get dressed. We'll be going to dinner in an hour.'

Without looking back, he strolled into one of the en suites, shut the door firmly behind him and stripped off his clothes.

His erection hadn't abated a touch.

The Cazorla family home was in a private enclave as exclusive as the one Raul's current house was in. As they neared it the coil in Charley's belly pulled ever tighter.

Of all the times to have to dine with her in-laws, now had to rank as the worst possible. All she wanted to do was lock herself away in a dark room, go to sleep, and pretend what had happened between her and Raul a few short hours ago had never occurred.

Her skin felt as sensitised as she'd ever known it, the movement of her clothes against her body heightening the sensations. Try as she might, she couldn't stop her eyes flittering to Raul's hands, those long, dark fingers holding the steering wheel like a caress, and imagining them running over her body and dipping between her legs...

When he'd gone for his shower, leaving her naked on the seat, the humiliation of it all had been almost too much to bear. That his intention had been to humiliate was all the spur she'd needed to drag herself up and into the other en suite. This had a surprisingly feminine feel to it with its soft, muted creams and whites; a total contrast to the rest of his vast room, which covered the entire top floor and was masculine to its core.

It was bad enough having come undone so thoroughly at his hands, or tongue to be precise, but she would not give him the satisfaction of thinking he'd bested her emotionally too.

Raul wanted her total subjugation. Hell would freeze over before she gave it to him. The only good thing she could cling to was that he hadn't bothered to tell her of their destination until they'd got into the car. Dining out was a way of life for him and she'd assumed they were off to yet another restaurant. On the nights he was home, which when they'd been properly married had been around fifty per cent of the time, they would both dress up and head out for the evening, sometimes with friends, sometimes just the two of them. It had reached the stage where she didn't think there was a restaurant in the whole of Barcelona she hadn't dined in.

'They do know I'm coming with you, don't they?' she asked for the second time, unable to believe how nervous she felt at the thought of being with his family again.

'I have no wish to provoke my mother to a heart attack,' he replied with a lazy smile. 'I can assure you, there is nothing for you to worry about. My family are nothing if not polite.'

That was true. One thing the entire Cazorla family did well was putting on a good front in any given situation.

The butler greeted them at the door, a discreet Englishman who had been with the family for years and had never once made any reference to the shared country he and Charley came from.

Lucetta and Marta Cazorla, Raul's mother and sister respectively, were in the drawing room awaiting their ar-

rival. Both were dressed impeccably, as if they were head-
ing off to a night at the opera, something Raul had once
taken Charley to and which, to her shame, she had fallen
asleep through.

She wondered when Raul would comment on her own
attire. He'd given her a sharp glance but hadn't said anything.

If she'd known they were coming here before she'd got
in the car, she would have made a greater effort than the
casual inky-coloured silk trousers with the tapered legs
and the silk blush-pink roll-neck top. On her feet were flat
snakeskin-effect sandals. She knew her outfit would hold
its own at any restaurant but in the Cazorla household…
she might as well have come dressed in her pyjamas.

It shouldn't matter to her. In the days after she'd left
she'd gone through her wardrobe and removed every item
that had been purchased for its suitability for Raul Cazorla's wife and not for personal style or comfort. She'd do-
nated ninety per cent of her wardrobe to charity and vowed
never to wear anything again that wasn't *her*.

All the same, Lucetta and Marta had always been good
to her, especially Marta, who, when Charley had first come
into Raul's life, had been tasked with the job of turning
Charley into a mini version of herself. Under Raul's direc-
tive, Marta had taken her to Barcelona's most exclusive
shopping arcade and had taken great delight in finding a
brand-new wardrobe for her.

Although not as direct in her enthusiasm for Raul's new
bride, Lucetta had gone out of her way to make Charley
feel a valued member of the family. Charley had never
been able to shake the feeling that Lucetta's friendliness
towards her was motivated by what she thought to be an
acceptable way to behave towards a daughter-in-law, rather
than out of any real affection. She would have treated the

Bride of Frankenstein with the same graciousness. But she had done her best to be welcoming and, for that, Charley would always have affection for her.

Dressing up and looking the part was something that mattered greatly to both Cazorla women, and for them Charley would have put on a dress and heels. Not silly heels that would leave her feet begging for mercy though. Three inches would have sufficed. Something to show she'd made an effort.

As it was, both faces lit up to see her walk through the door. If either was disappointed in her outfit or at seeing her again, it was hidden under a wave of perfumed embraces and air kisses.

An Adonis, a dry-sherry-based cocktail that was wonderfully moreish, was thrust into her hand by Marta, who linked her arm through Charley's with a grin.

'It is so good to see you,' she said, resting her head on Charley's shoulder. 'I always knew you'd see sense and come back to him.'

Charley met Raul's eyes and read the warning contained in them.

'It's lovely to see you too,' she answered, brushing aside the comment. She didn't want to lie to Marta, who had become a good friend, the two of them keeping in touch secretly after Charley had left Raul.

She took a sip, the taste reminding her of the time she and Marta had drunk so many of the cocktails before a meal they'd been unable to eat a bite, collapsing in giggles on a sofa much to the amusement of Raul and Marta's fiancé at the time, Fabio. Lucetta had been away, which had no doubt explained Marta's low inhibitions.

Raul had really taken care of her that night, she remembered. In the morning he'd handed her a glass of water and a couple of painkillers without a word of reproach, then climbed back into bed and held her, making sure not to squeeze her too tightly.

The tender memories sent a jolt through her.

Sometimes it was easy to only remember the bad stuff but there had been good times too, especially at the beginning.

Watching him now, chatting with his mother, she noticed the physical distance he kept between them. There was respect there but little affection.

After a few minutes of small talk, the wide dining-room door opened and Eduardo Cazorla, Raul's father, was wheeled through.

He looked exactly the same as when she'd last seen him, the left side of his face sagged and his hands arranged for him on his lap. Only his eyes, the same blue as his son and daughter's, showed any sign of life, letting you know that behind his infirmity lay a mind as sharp as the day the stroke had robbed him of his body.

When he caught sight of Charley, his eyes flickered to Raul, who did nothing but stare at his father with an expression that sent a shiver running up her spine. Goosebumps broke on her skin to see the same expression mirrored in his father's eyes.

Lucetta broke the ice, strolling to her husband and speaking to him in Spanish, her words too fast for Charley to understand anything but the gist of it, which seemed to be something along the lines of, 'Raul and Charley are back together.' As she explained the situation the butler entered the room to announce that dinner was ready.

Charley was placed opposite Raul and next to Marta, Lucetta next to her son. Eduardo sat in his usual place at the head of the table, his nurse, a young, dark-haired woman, by his side feeding him.

Seven courses were served in total. That was nothing;

if Lucetta hosted a 'proper' dinner party, a minimum of a dozen courses would be served. They started with gazpacho, which was followed by *calamares en su tinta*, squid in their own ink, which was far tastier than it sounded. As they ate, Raul, as he always did at these family meals, gave them a rundown on what was happening with the family business, the staff he had hired or fired, the hotel he'd closed for decontamination after an outbreak of the norovirus, the profit from the air fleet that was almost double the projected estimate...

And as he spoke, his words washing over her, Charley noticed how it all seemed to be aimed at his infirm father. And, for the first time, she noticed the challenge in the tone of his voice.

Because this was surely how he had always spoken to him. She'd just never noticed before how barbed his tone was or how pointed his stance.

For the first time it occurred to her that the Cazorlas, for all their outward respectability, were as dysfunctional as her own family.

There was Lucetta, the pillar of society.

Eduardo, the infirm head of the house.

Marta, the daughter with a mischievous streak that only came to the forefront when away from the stifling presence of her mother.

And Raul. The man who had to be the best at everything.

It was like observing a cleverly crafted game of manners in which everyone wore masks that hid anything resembling real emotion.

After a two-year absence from this table, it was as if Charley had sat down with a brand-new pair of eyes.

During her marriage she'd always felt intimidated in this house, terrified one of them would point a finger at her and expose her for being an imposter that no amount of expensive clothing or cosmetics could hide. Her fear had left her blind to what surrounded her.

The past two years had been a chance for her to find herself again and, no matter what happened in the future, she was determined never to lose herself again.

CHAPTER SEVEN

'WHEN DID YOU see my sister?' Raul asked, as soon as he had driven clear of the house.

She made no attempt to play innocent. 'Which time are you on about?'

So his hunch had been correct. It had been Marta's lack of curiosity about what Charley had been doing these past few years that had roused his suspicions. Even when their mother had left the room, Marta hadn't asked any of the questions he'd expected. It was because she'd already known the answers.

'It has been more than once?'

She sighed. 'I've seen her a handful of times since we split.'

'Am I correct in thinking this is something my mother is unaware of?'

'We thought it best not to tell her because we knew she'd feel obliged to tell you.'

That his mother certainly would have done.

'Who instigated it?'

'I did but it wasn't deliberate.' She turned her head to look at him. 'I went to see my father…'

'Your *father*?'

'He moved to Spain not long after we separated. He's living in a town on the Costa Dorado.'

'When you say he moved to Spain, how was he able to afford a property?' The last Raul had heard about his useless father-in-law was that he'd declared himself bankrupt after his latest get-rich scheme had failed.

'I bought a villa for him.' She didn't sound contrite about it. If anything, she sounded bullish.

'You bought a villa for him out of my money?'

'Technically it was my money. You gave it to me.'

'I can't believe you spent my money on buying that man a home.' Her father deserved nothing of the kind.

'I know you don't like him but he's my father.'

Raul took a deep breath. They were going off on a tangent here and he wanted to bring them back to the original thread of their conversation. But first he needed to make something clear. 'I do not dislike your father.'

Charley snorted her disbelief.

'What I have an issue with is the way he treated you and your mother when you were a child.' His fingers tightened on the steering wheel. 'He took advantage of your mother when she was seventeen years old and left her to raise you on her own giving little money and even less support.'

It used to infuriate him to think of how Graham Hutchinson had behaved towards his young family. The man had been fourteen years older than Charley's mother and, when he'd learned of the pregnancy, instead of doing the decent thing, had dumped her. He'd then flitted in and out of their lives as and when it had suited him, prioritising the two sons he had from a prior relationship. Charley and her mother had lived on the poverty line while Graham had taken exotic holidays and driven a sports car, thinking all his parental neglect could be made up for with expensive presents when he could afford them.

In truth, it still made him furious but he'd learned over the years that any criticism of Charley's father would be met with fierce indignation.

'That's all in the past,' she said now. Even through the

darkness of the night, he could sense her eyes blazing. 'I know he's no angel but he's still my dad and I love him. He needed a home and wanted to live closer to me. I had the money so I bought the villa for him.'

'So, he just happened to get in touch when he learned you'd left me and gave you his latest hard-luck story?'

'We've always kept in touch.'

There was that defensive tone again, but she made no comment about his guess that her father had gone to her cap in hand.

When they'd married, Graham had acted as though all his luck had rolled in at once, fully expecting his new son-in-law to support him. Raul had given him short shrift. After that, he'd kept his distance. As soon as Raul was out of the picture he'd swooped straight back in.

'So how does your father moving to Spain coincide with you visiting my sister?' he demanded to know, pulling them back on track.

'I went to visit my dad when he moved in and I dropped by to give Marta her books back,' she said.

'When did you borrow books from Marta?' He didn't think he'd ever seen Charley with a book in her hands.

'Lots of times. She thought it would help me learn Spanish if I read books in the language.'

'Why did you never tell me this?'

'I thought you'd laugh at me.'

'Why on earth would you think that?'

'You laughed at me whenever I tried to speak it.'

Had he? He'd always thought her attempts at speaking his language were cute. If he'd laughed it had been with pride that she was trying to master it. Had she really interpreted it as him making fun of her? 'I wasn't laughing at you.'

She didn't answer.

What did it matter anyway? Those days were gone.

'And after you dropped the books back, then what? You decided to carry on seeing each other?'

'It wasn't like that. I just got in the habit of meeting up with her whenever I visited my dad, that's all. We'd have a coffee and something to eat and then I'd leave. We were hardly conducting a high-level conspiracy.'

'Yet you kept it a secret from my mother. And from me.'

Raul shook his head, unable to believe the treachery conducted between his wife and sister. To think they'd been conspiring to see each other behind his back made his brain burn.

Where did family loyalty come into his sister's thinking? When Fabio had ended his relationship with Marta, Raul had been ready to kill him, not suggest they share cosy lunches together.

But then, Marta hadn't had loyalty drummed into her as he had. For Marta, childhood and life itself had been a charm; she'd been doted upon by the father who only spoke to his son to pick fault with him.

'Marta didn't want to upset you,' Charley said softly. 'She said you would think she was being disloyal.'

'You're damn right she was disloyal. But I'm not upset.'

'Then what are you?'

He forced his features into neutrality and glanced at her. 'I'm not anything.'

Silence rang out, not even a whisper of sound to be heard until Charley said, 'Nothing changes, does it?'

'What are you talking about?'

Her voice was sad. 'Nothing is allowed to be less than perfect, not even your own feelings.'

The silence suddenly filled with a roaring noise. It took a moment for him to realise the sound was in his own head.

His grip on the steering wheel tightened.

'How much did you have to drink tonight?' he asked, his voice tighter than he would like.

'See? Rather than confront what I've said, you deflect it.'

He expelled a long push of air from his lungs and flexed the tension from his fingers. He would not allow her to provoke him into an argument. All arguing did was bring about a loss of control, which solved nothing. Raul had learned that at a young age. His father had seen to that.

He remembered once sitting at the dining table while his father had read through his school report, slowly picking it apart, demanding to know why he'd only received the second highest grade on his end-of-year maths exam. Raul had argued his point that he'd spent the month leading up to that exam in bed with a bacterial infection but his reasons had been met with a fist thumped on the table and the school report had been ripped into pieces and burned. For his nerve in arguing back he'd received a two-week grounding. Nothing was mentioned about the top grades he'd received in all his other subjects.

Marta's report had been less than glowing academically but had been received by their father as if it were the best report ever written. Raul had been incensed at this double standard and, although Marta had begged him to keep quiet, he'd asked, reasonably, why they were being treated so differently. His insolence had been rewarded with an extra fortnight's grounding.

He'd been eleven.

'There's nothing to deflect,' he said, his vocal cords loosening under the force of his will. 'I'm perfectly in tune with my feelings.' To compound his point he flashed her a grin. 'Especially my baser ones.'

Charley undressed and quickly readied herself for bed while Raul made a phone call in his study.

She stared at the emperor-sized bed, at its plush seductiveness with the black sheets and plump pillows, inviting her to enter.

She wondered how many other women had been invited to enter it, before she could turn the thought away.

Turning the sheets back, she climbed in and lay down on her side of the bed. Strange to think that since leaving him she could have slept dead centre when in her own bed but had still favoured 'her' side.

She turned off the bedside light, flattened her pillow and burrowed herself into the sheets. The Spanish summer was hitting its stride but you wouldn't know it in this room where Raul had set the air conditioning to arctic.

Hopefully he would be kept busy making his phone calls and she would be fast asleep when he came up.

As was the contrary nature of sleep, it wouldn't come, her brain far too wired to switch off.

She found her mind turning over the evening's meal with his family. Maybe it was because she knew there was a time limit to the number of times she would share a meal with them but tonight she'd observed everything like a distant spectator, the fear of doing something wrong, something less than perfect, gone.

In all the years of their marriage she'd always thought Raul lucky to have such a close family and had envied him. How had she never noticed the undercurrent of poison there, especially between Raul and his father? Polite, gracious poison for sure, but poison all the same.

Her stomach clenched when she thought of her own family, the half-brothers she so wished would accept her as one of their own. What would Raul say if he learned she'd bought *them* a home each too? He'd accuse her of trying to buy their love and he would be right because that was exactly what she'd done. Except, as with everything else she did, she'd failed. She was more like her father than she'd ever thought possible. But she didn't want to be like him. She wanted to be like her mum, her sweet, naïve, hardworking mum who deserved everything good life had to offer.

She shut her eyes, trying to shake the direction of her thoughts and all the misery she'd thought she'd escaped when she'd married Raul, the man who'd made her feel like a princess even if only at the beginning...

A noise caught her attention and she heard the tread of his approach, followed by the creak of the bedroom door opening.

Squeezing her eyes together even more tightly, she concentrated on making her breathing deep and even. Hopefully he would assume she was asleep and leave her alone.

She heard him go into the bathroom, listened to the muffled sound of water running as he brushed his teeth. A slant of light came into the bedroom when he stepped back in, and she opened one eye a fraction. It took a few seconds for that eye to adjust to what it was seeing—Raul stripping off.

In the beat of a moment her mouth ran dry.

In no time at all he was down to his snug boxer shorts, his beautifully defined chest silhouetted against that tiny beam of light in all its glory; broad and hard, a smattering of dark hair running across his pecs and thickening the lower it ran...

Forget deep and even breathing. When his fingers hooked the sides of his boxers and tugged them off, pulling them past his strong thighs, all the air in her lungs went into hibernation.

His silhouette moved back to the bathroom and turned the light off, plunging the bedroom into darkness.

Too late she remembered her plan to feign sleep.

The bed dipped, the sheets rustled and a large, warm figure slid in beside her.

The dryness in her mouth became a memory as moisture filled it…and a lower part of her anatomy.

Immediately she pressed her thighs together in a futile attempt to counteract the heat filling between them and closed her eyes, anticipating the moment he reached out and pulled her to him.

Did she have the strength to even pretend lack of interest, when every part of her felt so heightened?

It felt as if she waited for ever for him to make his move, every passing minute dragging on to the next.

Nothing.

He lay on his side facing her, making her scold herself for not having faced the wall rather than the centre of the bed. She might have her eyes shut but she could feel his gaze upon her.

'Well?' she said, before she could stop her tongue from speaking. 'Isn't this the moment when you take your next payment?'

He shifted closer to her, his face near enough for her to feel the warmth of his minty breath.

'My payment is your body, whenever and wherever I require,' he said in a tone that washed through her skin like a caress, moving even closer so the tip of his nose pressed against hers.

Her lips parted in anticipation of his kiss.

'But tonight I will put my payment on hiatus.' Suddenly he twisted away and turned his back to her. 'Unless you wish to make a payment to me of your own accord?' he added, pulling the sheets over his shoulder and edging away from her.

'That will never happen,' she whispered, goosebumps covering her at the abrupt withdrawal of his warmth.

'Never say never.' He laughed quietly. 'If you change your mind…'

'Dream on.'

'Oh, I will.'

Raul smiled into his pillow and closed his eyes. He could practically smell her frustration.

When he *did* make love to her, she would be desperate for his touch. All her defiance would be smothered by desire.

He let his mind run free, imagining all the ways he would take her and she would take him; imagined her tongue snaking its way down his chest…

But something else fought for space in his head, the same something that had been jarring in his throat since the journey back home.

Her words echoed within him, becoming louder the more he tried to push them away.

'Nothing is allowed to be less than perfect—not even your own feelings.'

Was there some truth in it?

No. Of course there wasn't. Charley was trying to needle him.

A memory flashed in his mind of one time he *had* allowed his emotions to get the better of him. It had been the night Charley told him she didn't want his baby.

His anger had been bubbling at the surface, impossible to hide and, for the first time in his adult life, he'd given into it, lashing out verbally, cruelly. He'd called her a gold-digging bitch and told her to leave, not meaning it and never for a moment imagining she would.

It hadn't been one-sided. The recriminations had flown both ways, Charley screaming back at him with furious tears streaming down her face that their marriage had no basis in reality, that he patronised her and treated her like a child, that he should find himself another wife, some-one who could breed a dozen children for him, look per-fect and run a multinational company and all in her sleep. That he was a cold, arrogant control freak.

By the time the anger had notched down to a simmer, both of them visibly calmer, her bags were packed.

'This is ridiculous,' he'd said. 'You're not going any-where.'

'You told me to leave,' she'd replied with a face so stony it was like looking at a statue.

'That was in the heat of the moment and now I'm tell-ing you to stay.'

'But I don't want to stay.' She'd looked straight at him with eyes that were a red, raw mess, black streaks of make-up splotched down her cheeks. At that moment she had looked exactly as he'd felt. 'I can't live like this any more.'

And just like that, their marriage was over.

He almost laughed at the irony. The one time in his adulthood that he'd truly given into his feelings, his wife had walked out on him.

If that didn't tell him he was right to keep his emotions controlled and locked away, nothing did.

The grounds of the building Raul had purchased to rehome Poco Rio were filled with overgrown weeds dying in the heat and parched grass. Charley didn't care; all she saw in her mind's eye was how glorious it would be when the renovations were complete.

The architect, a middle-aged man with a shock of white hair called Vittore, had travelled from Barcelona with them. Other than Raul's introduction, the two men had conversed between themselves during the short heli-copter trip and even shorter car journey, discussing other business projects they were working on together. If Vittore was bothered about travelling to Valencia on a Saturday morning there was no sign of it in his relaxed demeanour.

She itched to get back inside the sprawling one-storey building; she had been dreaming of this moment for two long months. Of course, her dreams hadn't involved Raul buying the place in his name. In her dreams it had been in her name and, when all the renovations were complete, she'd intended to sign it over to Poco Rio so they never need worry about losing their home again.

He'd said he *might* give her the deeds if she proved herself to him. All she could do was try.

The main thing was that so long as she kept her side of the bargain and stayed with him for four months, Raul would keep his and Poco Rio would have a new home. That much she trusted him on.

The interior of the pretty red stone building, which was so much nicer than the institutionalised building Poco Rio was currently homed in, was as ramshackle as she remembered, but that was only decoration. The rooms were large and, once new windows had been installed, would be airy.

'I'm going to look around and see what my money has bought,' Raul said, leaving her with Vittore.

The moment he was out of sight, Charley sat on the dusty floor, opened her briefcase and pulled out her plans. 'Please don't feel I am treading on your toes,' she said, speaking in hesitant Spanish, 'but here's a guide to what the centre needs.'

Vittore squatted beside her and took the plans. After he'd perused them for a while, he said, 'Is there a reason the doorways need to be so wide?'

'A lot of the children have wheelchairs,' she answered carefully, scared of things being lost in translation.

He nodded thoughtfully, then asked her some more questions.

They were deep in conversation, Charley pointing out where she thought a wall should be knocked down to make a large soft-play area, when Raul rejoined them.

Her Spanish died on her lips.

He regarded her for a moment, his eyes drilling into her with something that looked like cold suspicion, before turning to Vittore. 'Has Charlotte explained the brief?'

Vittore nodded and stretched back up. 'Her plans are very impressive.' He turned his attention to her. 'Be proud. You have done well.'

Charley's cheeks flushed at the unexpected compliment.

She hadn't expected *that*.

She became even more flustered when Vittore carefully refolded her plans along the seams she'd made and tucked them into his large carry-case. 'Next time, you roll them.'

'Sorry?' She didn't have the faintest idea what he was talking about.

'Next time you create plans, roll them, don't fold.'

She bit into her bottom lip to stop the smile that fought to spread over her face. Vittore was a renowned architect with over twenty years' experience and he was complimenting and advising her as if she were, if not an equal, then a promising student.

So stunned was she that the rest of the conversation passed her by, right until the moment came for them to leave.

While Raul and Vittore headed outside, she gave the place one last look, imagining how bright and fabulous it would be when the renovations and subsequent decoration were complete. Her heart swelled to think of the children's faces when they saw it for the first time.

The humidity outside hung heavy like a damp cloak and Charley was grateful to get back in the helicopter, where the air conditioning ran at full blast. She caught the tail end of the men's conversation and Vittore saying he would bring a team over on Monday. He smiled encouragingly at Charley and added to Raul, 'Your wife's plans have made our job much easier.'

'You are going to follow them?'

'As much as we can. They make a lot of sense.'

Raul's gaze caught hers. 'My wife has hidden talents.'

His tone and expression were so inscrutable she didn't know if he was being serious or mocking her.

CHAPTER EIGHT

Soon they were back in Barcelona making the short drive to the villa. Saturdays in the city were always busy, especially in summer, and today was no exception, so, while traffic was calmer during the weekend, the number of pedestrians more than made up for it.

The villa was empty when they got in; the household staff all took weekends off.

During their marriage Charley had lived for the weekends. Sharing a home with staff was something she'd never got used to. One of many things she'd struggled with. Going from a tiny two-bedroom flat in a high-rise block of flats in south-east London to an eight-bedroom villa by the sea would have challenged anyone.

She thought of Raul's parents' household with a shudder. They had live-in staff on call seven days a week.

'Vittore was impressed with your plans,' Raul commented as he headed into the kitchen and found the capsules to slot into the coffee machine.

She managed a nod, still stunned at the praise she'd received from the architect.

Other than entertain kids, she'd never done *anything* in her life that warranted praise before. It was a heady feeling to know she didn't have to fail at everything she set her mind to.

She thought back wistfully to the businesses she'd tried

so hard at but for which she'd never been able to find the magic quality Raul possessed with all *his* businesses. She'd so badly wanted to make him proud and for him to see her as his equal, and all she'd done was mess it up, over and over again. The pressure had been too great to bear.

'Where did you learn how to do it?' he asked.

'I did a search on the Internet on how to create plans. The estate agent did a scale floor plan so I worked from that.'

He pulled two china cups out of the cupboard, placing one in the slot of the machine. 'I'm sorry I dismissed your plans the other day.'

Her heart jolted at this unexpected apology. She hadn't thought the word sorry was in his vocabulary.

'That's okay,' she said with a shrug. 'I'm used to it.'

He looked at her curiously. 'What do you mean by that?'

'You used to cross-examine me about everything to do with my businesses. I always knew you didn't take my plans or ideas seriously.'

'I took them seriously enough to give you a lot of money to pay for them.'

She sighed. 'But I always knew you were humouring me.'

Raul punched the button on the machine at the same moment a swell of anger cut through him. 'I was not humouring you. I wanted you to succeed and I believed you could. But, Charlotte, you left school without any qualifications. All I did was give you the benefit of my knowledge and experience. It was when you chose to ignore my advice that your businesses floundered.'

It had been hard for him to watch her throw them all away, discarding them as if they were toys that had lost their sparkle after their first few uses. But he'd kept his patience, as hard as it had been. A part of him had admired her guts in dusting herself off and starting again.

It wasn't until he'd lost that tolerance and witnessed her immediate horrified refusal to have a child that he'd realised her businesses had failed *because* she'd treated them like toys. They'd been something for her to play with so she could put off the moment she confessed to not wanting his child that bit longer, enabling her to milk him and their lifestyle for all it was worth.

He'd understood all this the night she'd left him and still he'd asked her to stay.

What sickened him more than anything was knowing he would have taken her back, right up until the divorce papers had landed on his doorstep.

He'd almost lost control of himself that day too, had taken his car for a drive, not knowing where he was going and somehow ending up in Valencia. Before he'd known it, he'd been at the street listed on the divorce papers.

The fog had lifted and he'd slammed on his brakes before he could seek her house out, a cold sweat breaking out on his skin.

He was certain the tyre marks at the entrance of her street had been made by him when he'd spun the Lotus round and screeched away.

Thinking about how she'd played him sent another spike of fury through him. He tempered it by the skin of his teeth.

'It was hard for me,' she said quietly, leaning against the wall by the door and folding her arms across her chest. 'I was desperate to impress you.'

'What for? You were my wife. I wouldn't have married you if I wasn't already impressed by you.'

'You were impressed with my body,' she answered with a hard laugh.

'It was more than that and you know it,' he cut in. 'I admired your spirit.' Something which, he had to admit now he thought of it, had disappeared during the latter years of their marriage.

How had he not noticed?

Seeing that spirit return now, that zinging feistiness, sent the most peculiar feeling of déjà vu tearing through him.

'I wanted you to be impressed with my mind and my abilities,' she said, a rueful twinge to her voice. 'But it was so much harder than I thought it would be. Call me naïve but I wanted to do things my own way, to prove I could do it, but I put so much pressure on myself that I crumbled. It didn't help that I didn't speak the language.'

'You've mastered it well enough since we separated.' He'd employed a tutor to help her with Spanish but after a few months she'd put a stop to the lessons, saying they were too hard. Like driving a car, she'd mastered Spanish after she'd left him and without his help. 'I suppose reading Marta's books helped.'

'Not much. It was working at Poco Rio that really did it. The kids hardly speak Spanish never mind English so I had to learn fast if I wanted them to understand me.'

Raul didn't answer, his teeth clenching together as they always did whenever he thought of her surrounded by small children on a daily basis.

Charley loved children.

But not as much as she loved money...

Was that really true? All the evidence pointed to her leading a frugal existence without him. And she hadn't asked for any money for herself...

She'd lapsed into silence, her head bowed. Then suddenly she lifted her chin and stared at him with enough force to keep his focus on her and not the coffee machine.

'Marrying you was all wrong,' she said, her eyes wide. 'You were the shining star turning the family business from silver into gold—*everything* you touched turned into gold. Everything I touched turned into rust. I couldn't compete.'

'Our marriage wasn't a competition.'

'I know, but for me…'

'For you, what?' he asked, when her words tailed off.

'I wasn't equipped to deal with any of it. I tried, really, I did, but I knew you wanted perfection. Never mind learning Spanish, you wanted me to speak proper English, to wear the right clothes, to be a wife you could be proud to have on your arm…'

'That was *not* how it was,' he retorted, irked she could twist things round to make herself seem like some kind of victim. 'I was trying to help you fit in with my world.'

'I wanted to fit in too and it took me a long time to realise that I couldn't because I *don't* belong. The world I come from is just too different. You make everything you touch turn into pure gold, but all you could do with me was add gold-plating—underneath I was still Charley, not the Charlotte you tried to create.'

'That's a good story you've spun there but my memory tells it differently. In all the time we were together not once did you say you were unhappy. Not once.'

'That's because I was terrified that if I said how I felt, you would agree with me. I spent most of our time together waiting for the day you realised I wasn't up to scratch and replaced me with a better model.'

She looked and sounded so sincere he almost believed her. 'Answer me this. In all the time we were together did I *ever* give you cause to think I would cheat on you?'

She shook her head. 'I always knew you'd never cheat, you're too honourable. But,' she added, before he could

retaliate, 'you spend a huge amount of your time in hotels and on cruise liners surrounded by beautiful, well-
bred women throwing themselves at you. Knowing you
wouldn't cheat didn't mean I was stupid enough to believe
someone else wouldn't catch your eye and you'd want to
get to know them better. I knew I was disposable, just as
Jessica was disposable when I came back on the scene.'

Dios, she could not be serious.

'Why would you even *think* such a thing?' he demanded
to know, not giving her time to answer before adding, 'I
never once looked at another woman in the whole time
we were married.'

Doubt reverberated through her curvaceous frame.

The incongruity was laughable. Charley had been the
one to walk out. She'd left *him*. Their marriage vows had
clearly meant a damn sight more to him than they had to
her.

'Why would I have looked at another woman when I
had you to come home to?' he said, striding over to her
and pressing a hand against the wall by her head. 'You,
cariño, are all woman.'

She tensed, her jaw becoming rigid as she swallowed.
'You've just proven everything I've said. You really *do*
think I'm only good for one thing.'

'And that, I can assure you, you are superb at.'

She grabbed his wrist and tried to yank it down, but he
twisted his hand and caught her own wrist, pinning her
without any effort, then snaked an arm around her waist
and pulled her flush to him.

Her head tilted back, her green eyes staring at him with
the strangest mixture of contempt and desire. 'When did
you become so cruel?'

'When I realised the woman I adored was playing me
for a fool.' And with that, he brought his mouth down to

hers, drowning out the voices in his head clamouring to argue with this assessment of her.

Charley tried to resist. She closed her mouth as tightly as she could, tried to shut her senses off, but it was like fighting the tide.

His heat, his scent, filled her, creeping through the pores of her skin and down into her blood.

She could push him away. All it would take was one hard shove and she'd be free. Raul might be many things but he would never use his physical strength to force her to do anything she didn't want.

But they had a deal. She was here for his pleasure and no other reason.

And, if she was being honest with herself, she was here for her own pleasure too because her husband set her alive in a way she would never have known if they'd never met.

Rationality fighting with her senses, she put a hand to his chest, still uncertain if she was going to push or pull. Her fingers splayed against him and before she knew it she'd gripped his shirt. Her lips softened and parted as she melted into him.

His kiss was hard, demanding, his tongue moving within her, her own dancing against it.

Her grip on his shirt loosened and she wound her arms up and around his neck, her fingers pressing into the back of his head, leaning against his strength as he kissed her so thoroughly she doubted she would have been able to stand if he weren't there supporting her.

Time became nothing. All she knew and all she cared about was now, this moment, and the heat burning through her.

His kisses deepened, then he broke away long enough to dip his head and nip her neck.

Then his hands clasped her bottom and she was pushed against the wall while simultaneously lifted off the ground.

Wrapping her legs around his waist, she pressed kisses over his face, tasting him, inhaling him, rubbing her nose into the smooth skin of his cheeks that roughened as she nuzzled his jawline.

He held her tightly to him, as if her weight meant nothing, and carried her through the kitchen to the narrow stairs. She had no idea how he managed to make it up the two flights with her in his arms, could only assume the fever burning through them drove him onwards until he kicked open their bedroom door and threw her effortlessly onto the bed. Stepping back, Raul gazed down at her, his handsome features taut, his chest surging. Her heart thrummed painfully, pulses racing through her as she stared right back.

Without a word, his eyes holding hers, he pulled at his belt to undo it then opened the buttons and dropped his trousers.

In reply, she raised herself enough to tug off her top and throw it onto the floor.

Working methodically, Raul undid the buttons of his shirt while Charley fumbled with the zip of her denim shorts before kicking them off and sending them sailing towards the other clothes that were forming a messy pile by his feet. His shirt joined them, leaving him in nothing but boxer shorts that stretched over his snake hips and tight buttocks, the strain of his erection visible through the fabric...

Heat bubbled deep within her, a sweet yet torturous sensation that begged for attention, and she dragged herself to her knees, taking in every part of him from his toes to his cropped dark hair as she unclasped her bra and threw it to one side, not caring where it landed. Then, finally, she pulled her underwear down past her hips, as Raul's eyes watched every move she made, his strong throat moving as he swallowed.

'Lie down,' he instructed, his words guttural.

She did as she was bid and laid back, posing provocatively for him with one arm hooked over her head, a hand clasping a breast that was practically crying for attention, deliberately encircling a hard nipple.

A muted groan came from his throat and he yanked at his boxers and tugged them down past his muscular thighs, freeing his erection.

More moisture filled her, the heated ache in the apex of her thighs now nothing but a mass of sensation begging for his touch.

A warning thought rang out, breaking through the haze.

'I'm not on the pill any more,' she managed to gasp, beyond caring if this gave away her total lack of sex-life since their parting.

His blue eyes widened a touch before darkening, his desire as easy to read as anything she'd ever seen before.

Wrenching his gaze from her, he took the three steps to his dresser and opened the top shelf, rummaging for a moment before producing a packet of condoms.

She couldn't deny the relief at seeing the box still in its seal.

Raul used his teeth to rip the clear seal off, then pulled a foil square out of the box and ripped it open.

They hadn't used condoms since their engagement. Her heart twisted to see him struggle with it, as if he were out of practice…

All thoughts vanished when he turned to her and feasted his eyes on her naked form. 'Spread your legs.'

Parting her thighs, she exposed herself to him, thrilling in the dilation of his eyes as he drank her in, then strode over to her and climbed on the bed, grabbing her hands and pinning them beside her head, his fingers entwining in hers.

His mouth crashed down on hers, crushing her lips, his tongue sweeping into her mouth while the tip of his erection found the heart of her and, with one long thrust, he pushed into her, filling her whole.

Charley could no more hold back her cry of relief than she could swim to the moon.

Raul's hold on her hands tightened as he moved within her with no hesitation, no lingering caresses, just pure carnality.

She parted her legs ever wider, her pelvis tilted so they ground together, taking everything he gave and giving it back with sobs of pleasure. Sensation fizzed and built within her, heightening with every stroke.

The feel of him on her and inside her, his powerful thrusts, the way his chest crushed her breasts, everything fused together to form one whole sensitised buzz forming into a tight ball that, with one long final stroke, exploded within her. Raul's groan of release toppled her over the edge.

She clung to him, her hands, freed from his hold, clasping his head as she buried her face in his neck, whimpering into his skin as pulsations rippled through her.

For the longest time they lay together, her legs wrapped around his waist, Charley savouring the feeling of release and the weight of his body upon her.

But all too soon he shifted off her and padded to the bathroom, leaving her alone for long enough that the glowing feeling deep inside her dimmed.

This means nothing. He hates you. He thinks you're a gold-digger. He didn't even want to hear how you felt during your marriage, he cared only about getting you naked.

She pushed the thoughts away, refusing to acknowledge the way her heart felt as if someone had grabbed hold of it and given it a mighty squeeze.

Silently he returned, climbed back under the sheets and pulled her into his arms. He dropped a kiss to her forehead.

Her heart twisted as she listened to his deepening breaths, his hand remaining buried in her hair as he fell into sleep.

It didn't matter what he believed or that he hadn't listened to her. It wasn't as if they were intending to give their marriage another go in the proper fashion.

She was here for his pleasure, nothing more. And that meant *her* pleasure too.

Things were already different between them. It *felt* different and not just because she'd been blackmailed into being here. The dynamic between them had changed. In a sick kind of way, it was better like this, more honest. She didn't have to mask who she was any more; her fear of disappointing him was gone.

She should be celebrating. Four months of physical bliss without having to pretend to be someone she wasn't?

In other words, exactly what their marriage should have been.

Charley was sitting at her desk in the office adjoining Raul's, trying to read a book on finance while nibbling at a biscuit.

'You look as if you have a headache,' he said, walking through the open doorway to join her, two cups of coffee in his hands.

'Just trying to get my head around it all.' She wiped the crumbs off her blouse onto her desk, then swept them into her hand and into the bin.

Raul had been as good as his word. All week she'd been

chained to his side. Monday and Tuesday had been spent in his office, Wednesday and Thursday in France where he was involved in negotiations to have a base for his air fleet in Paris. He'd been incredibly busy, in and out of meetings, most of which he'd insisted she come along to, working at a pace that made her dizzy.

Today they were back in Barcelona and, while the pace seemed no less frantic, there was an air of calm about the place, his staff more relaxed. It was probably that Friday feeling, she guessed. It had infected her too, that sense of the working week being almost over and a couple of days of relaxation to look forward to.

She hated to admit it, but the thought of a weekend alone with him sent a thrill through her.

Making love to Raul was as addictive as the packet of biscuits she'd been munching her way through. Having his throat, so strong and golden, in her eyeline right now as he took the seat opposite her...

'This book might as well be gibberish,' she said, closing it with a snap and pushing it over to him.

He raised a dark brow and loosened his tie. 'The main reason your businesses went bust was because you didn't take care of the bottom line. Unless you want the same thing to happen at Poco Rio, I suggest you pay attention carefully.'

'But Poco Rio is different,' she protested.

'A business is a business. Catering for children is no different from any other business—the bottom line is still the same.'

'Not in this case...'

Her phone went off, jumping with the vibrations from the alert. She snatched it up.

'Who is it?'

'My dad.'

'What does he want?'

'He's replying to a message I left for him last week.' She winced at her slip that she'd been waiting a week to hear back from him and hurriedly added, 'I wanted to know when he's free for lunch.'

His expression was even. 'Are you forgetting our deal? Your place is by my side.'

She rolled her eyes. 'Not for a second. That's why I suggested he choose a weekend.'

'You're still by my side at weekends.'

'Even prisoners are allowed visitation rights.' She took a sip of her coffee.

A pulse worked at his jaw.

'You're not seriously thinking you can stop me visiting my family?' she asked. 'Because that would make you even more hateful.'

His eyes crinkled at the edges. 'You didn't think I was hateful last night when I made you come with my tongue.'

'You're very talented,' she responded sweetly, wishing her face didn't flush at the memory.

'Why don't you sit on my lap and I'll show you how talented I am with something other than my tongue?' He placed his chin on his hand and held his blue eyes on her, a lascivious glimmer in them.

'Why do I get the feeling you're trying to distract me again? We were talking about my dad, not about having sex in your office.' She had to admit, the thought of doing something *here*, in the heart of his empire, sent the most erotic charge racing through her.

He clicked his tongue on the roof of his mouth and settled back in his chair, cradling his cup to him, that same glimmer still there in his eyes. 'No, I wouldn't try and stop you seeing your father, even though I could.'

Oh, yes, he could. Of that Charley had no doubts. But

she wondered if he would still hold the kids of Poco Rio over her head like a weapon if he actually met them and spent time with them.

'It concerns me to see you give up a day for something that might not happen,' he continued. 'Your father is hardly the most reliable of people.'

'Your concern for my emotional well-being is touching.'

Something dark glittered across his features. 'I know you dislike criticism of him but I spent three years watching you be disappointed by that man.'

Her hackles rose. 'That *man* is my father.'

'And if he had ever acted like a father towards you I would be more forgiving of him. Charlotte, he was an hour late for our wedding. Your mother had to walk you down the aisle.'

'He was stuck in traffic,' she snapped, her belly knotting at the remembrance.

'If he'd left earlier traffic wouldn't have been a problem.'

'You have no right,' she said, red-hot fury pushing through her. 'No right at all, not when your own family is more screwed up than mine.'

'My family is—'

'Perfect,' she finished for him. 'The famous Cazorlas, practically perfect in every way, apart from the only son clearly hating the infirm father and having a strained relationship with the mother, the only daughter hiding the essence of herself when with the parents so as not to fall off the pedestal they've put her on, everyone putting on a front when they step out of the door because nothing's more important than showing that *perfect face*.'

The tendons on Raul's neck were straining, his jaw clenched. 'I warn you now, Charlotte, stop.'

'Oh, I get it—it's okay for you to pick fault with *my* family but I'm not allowed to criticise yours?'

'You don't know what you're talking about.'

'Yes, I do—I lived with you for three years, remember? The difference now is that I'm not wrapped up in my own insecurities. I can see it all clearly.'

He got to his feet and placed his hands on the desk, looming down over her, his face a mask. 'My family is none of your business, not any more. You lost that right when you walked out on me.'

'Then consider my family off limits too.'

His eyes bored into her, his lips now a tight line. 'What date has your father given for you to meet?'

Her answer was just as terse. 'A week on Saturday.'

'I will check my diary and let you know if we're free.'

'Thank you.'

He straightened and reached for his cup, his breathing heavy. 'I've arranged for a member of the finance team to sit down with you for the afternoon and go through some accounts with you.'

'Now?'

'Now.'

He strode back into his adjoining office and closed the door behind him.

CHAPTER NINE

RAUL PASSED THE living room on his way outside for his daily swim and paused.

Charley was sprawled on the sofa thumbing through a Spanish magazine, dressed in a thigh-length white T-shirt, her hair pulled back into a loose ponytail, not a scrap of make-up on her face. She was working her way mechanically through a bar of chocolate.

Deep in concentration, she didn't notice his presence, allowing him to gaze at her unhindered.

His guts twisted.

Walking away before she noticed him, he stepped out into the swimming-pool area, placed his towel on a sun lounger, and dived in.

As he powered his way through the water he waited for the usual calm to envelop him and empty his mind.

Today, it didn't happen. Length after length, his mind was filled with his wife. Not the heated discussion about their families that had taken place two days ago and which had settled into a strange kind of truce, nor their lovemaking, the potency of which still showed no sign of abating, but the vision of her sitting on that sofa eating the chocolate bar, just as she'd been eating those biscuits at her desk.

It was that sense of déjà vu again, that feeling of staring at the Ghost of Wife Past.

For the first time, he properly considered if there could

be any truth in her words that she had spent their marriage unhappily striving to be the person she thought he wanted.

When they'd first met she'd had an innate sunniness. Smiles and laughter had come easily. They were what had drawn him to her, along with the earthy sexiness that came off her in waves.

While the smiles and laughter were no more evident now than they had been by the end of their marriage, the earthiness had returned.

He'd assumed the casual way she'd dressed when they'd first met had been due to her lack of money, had assumed that all women wanted personal shoppers, hairdressers, beauticians and dieticians on speed-dial. His mother and sister did; all his exes had. He'd never met *any* woman who didn't.

But then, he'd never met a woman like Charley before. His inner circle was insular, he acknowledged, filled with like-minded people with the same wealth and outlook on life.

Charley had embraced it all, he reminded himself, right down to the rationing of chocolate.

All he'd wanted was for her to be happy and fit into his world and, with a little help, she'd fitted in perfectly. With his help she'd never had to feel that anyone was judging her. Or so he'd believed…

To see her eating a bar of chocolate…it was such a small thing, but enough to shift his perspective even more. Enough to make him question…

Gone was the haute couture. Gone, the immaculately coiffured hair. Gone, the rigid diet. Gone too, were the rock-hard abs she'd developed during their marriage, re-placed with the luscious softness he recalled from their early days.

When he'd completed his daily two hundred lengths,

he hauled himself out of the pool. For once there were no hunger pangs. Everything felt tight inside him, far too tight to eat.

He grabbed his towel and rubbed it over his hair and face. As he towelled the water from his back Charley came out into the morning sunshine and walked over to him, her phone in hand.

'Have we got anything planned for tomorrow?' she asked, keeping a respectable distance from him although he noted with some satisfaction that her eyes lingered on his chest for longer than was respectable. All at once, the disquiet within him evaporated. He closed the distance and reached for her hips.

'You'll get me wet,' she scolded but with definite half-heartedness. After a week of erotic lovemaking, he knew her resistance was nothing but a measure to prove her own self-control against him.

'That's the idea,' he murmured. Unable to resist, he pulled her in for a kiss, delighting in the sweet, chocolate taste of her mouth.

She sighed into him, slipping her tongue into his mouth and sliding her arms around his neck, before her hands balled into fists and she stepped away. A dark, wet stain now marked her top.

'Tomorrow?' she reminded him.

'You will be with me.'

'Doing what though? Anything important or am I going to be stuck in my office again?'

'Doing whatever I require.'

'Seve's just messaged me.' Her speech came in a rush. 'Two of the staff at Poco Rio have caught a sickness bug.'

'And that involves you how?'

'They're going to be short-staffed.'

'No.'

'I haven't asked for anything yet,' she protested.

'Do I have to remind you that our deal is for you to stay by my side?'

'No, but if they don't have the staff, the centre won't be able to open and the children...'

He did not want to hear a single word about children, not from her lips.

Every time she uttered the word he was reminded of her treachery.

'I'm not prepared to debate the matter. We have already agreed that your day-to-day work at the centre is over.'

Her face darkened, her eyes ringing with obvious contempt. 'But—'

'Shh.' He placed a finger to her lips. 'It's a beautiful day with no work or anything else to worry about. Let's not waste it by arguing about things we have already agreed on.'

Gently he moved his finger off her mouth and traced it down her neck.

He could see her thinking, her eyes moving as she deliberated his words. When his fingers found the band holding her hair back and carefully tugged it out, to let her hair fall down across her shoulders, her breath hitched. When his lips reclaimed hers, there was no more protest. Only willingness. Followed by ecstasy.

After a day spent making love and a night spent doing the same all over again, Raul awoke on Monday morning to an empty bed and the distant sound of a helicopter flying close by.

He stretched and looked at his watch, surprised to see he'd overslept by a good hour. He could have sworn he'd set his alarm.

Wondering where Charley had got to, he showered and

dressed quickly. He had a meeting with the MD of his air fleet at ten a.m. and if there was one thing Raul did not appreciate, it was tardiness, either from others or himself.

The scent of fresh coffee and newly baked *bollos*—sweet rolls—pervaded the air: morning aromas that never failed to lift his spirits. The household staff worked at their chores with their customary zeal. The dining table had been set...

Set for one.

On the placemat sat a folded letter.

Eyes wide with disbelief, he read it.

Gone to the centre. Back some time this evening.
Charley.
PS: Have borrowed the helicopter.

Of all the reactions provoked by the note, the one that came to the forefront the quickest was laughter.

He could scarcely credit her nerve.

That feeling of witnessing the Ghost of Wife Past consumed him again. The Charley he'd first met had been impulsive, living for the moment...

But surely she must know what the consequences would be?

The laughter died as quickly as it had come. By the time his *café con leche* and *bollos* were brought through to him, all amusement had gone.

Did she seriously think she could take off to the centre in direct contravention of his wishes?

Was she seriously serious, as she herself would have put it?

Did she think that now she was back in his bed she could do as she pleased and he would be as forgiving as he had always been?

It was time his wife learned a lesson. If she refused to learn it then he would cancel their agreement and to hell with the day care centre. It meant nothing to him anyway.

Raul parked the Lotus next to the minibus Charley had been driving the week before and stared at the institutional-looking building with the same distaste as when he'd first been there.

When he'd called his helicopter back to Barcelona, his pilot had been full of contrition.

It hadn't taken Raul long to put the pieces together. Charley had got the pilot's number from the household directory and said she wanted to go to Valencia. The pilot hadn't thought twice about the instruction. He would think twice if Charley tried the same stunt again.

Raul assumed she'd turned his alarm clock off at some point during the night in the snatches of sleep he'd managed between bouts of lovemaking.

He had to press his thumb on a buzzer at the door and wait for someone to approve his admittance before he could enter. When he was finally granted entry, his initial reaction was that he'd walked into a clinic.

To his mind, day care centres were supposed to be bright and colourful places full of squealing children. The exterior might have an institutional feel to it, but he'd expected the interior to be more fitting, not grey and lifeless.

The man he recognised as Seve greeted him at the door of a large room that looked more as he'd imagined, filled with colourful drawings and bright furniture. He could smell food cooking and the aroma was not at all unpleasant.

Seve shook his hand enthusiastically, treating Raul as if Elvis himself had walked into the building. 'It is an honour to meet you. We are all so grateful for what you have done for the children here. It is an amazing thing.'

As Seve droned on Raul took stock of what surrounded him. The harder he looked, the harder his heart pumped and the lighter his head felt.

Of the dozen or so children in the room at least half were in wheelchairs. All of them sat in a horseshoe around a woman dressed in a bright yellow all-in-one outfit, bright red curly wig and a round red nose. The woman was juggling soft balls, while standing on a plank of wood atop a football. Her balance looked precarious, her juggling atrocious—she dropped more balls than she caught—but it made no difference to the children, all of whom watched with rapt attention, some of them squealing their laughter loudly.

It took a few moments for his brain to comprehend that it was Charley in the ridiculous clown outfit.

A small hand tugged at his arm and he looked down to see a young boy gazing up at him.

'This is Ramon,' Seve said, with a benevolent smile. 'I think he wants you to watch the show with him.'

'I'm not here for the entertainment,' Raul said, intending to add, 'I'm here to take Charley home.' But when he opened his mouth to say the words, he caught Ramon's eye and was rewarded with a smile that could melt the entire Arctic Circle.

Somehow Raul allowed himself to be guided over to the floor by the child who, it was obvious, had Down's syndrome. As he looked at the other faces one thing was abundantly clear—every single one of these children was severely disabled. One other thing was clear though too: every single one of these children was enthralled with the performance Charley was giving them.

Suddenly she spotted him and for a moment she faltered. When the balls fell out of her hand this time, there was nothing feigned about it.

A girl who looked to be no more than eight, who had the most beautiful curly white-blonde hair, toddled over to Raul, her head turned to one side, and stared with curiously vacant eyes, then prodded a finger into his cheek.

'Leave the nice man alone, Karin,' Seve said, scooping the little girl up into his arms. Karin thus proceeded to poke Seve in the face.

'Sorry about that,' Seve said, gently taking Karin's hands to stop any more incessant prodding. 'She doesn't know what she's doing.'

'It's no problem.' Other than a slightly tilted head, there was nothing Raul could see physically atypical about the little girl. But something clearly wasn't quite right.

Charley had stopped juggling and was now making balloon animals in the same slapstick manner that had most of the children, those who could, laughing. When she spoke it was in precise Spanish without any of the inhibitions she'd displayed when speaking the language to Vittore.

She finished her act with a bow, then Seve and two other workers took on the task of wheeling and walking the children into an adjoining room that looked, from where Raul sat, like a dining room, while Charley gathered her props together in a battered old suitcase.

She didn't say a single word to him. If he hadn't caught her eye during her little show, he would have thought she hadn't noticed him.

Done packing, she picked up the suitcase and carried it off. Raul followed her out of the room and into the entrance hall, where she turned off down a connecting corridor and opened the door into a large storeroom.

'I'm sorry, okay?' she muttered, stacking the suitcase

upright next to a shelving unit crammed with waterproof paints, non-toxic glues and all manner of child-friendly crafts.

For once, he was at a loss for what to say.

Charley pulled her red nose off, followed by the wig, which was making her scalp itch.

A part of her had known Raul would turn up. Never mind her defiance, borrowing his helicopter would have tipped him over the edge.

A part of her had *wanted* him to follow her, to see the children for himself, to understand how important the project was on a humane level.

As vain as she knew it to be, another part of her wished he had come when she hadn't been dressed as a clown in pyjamas.

She wished he would say something.

She unzipped the yellow onesie and stepped out of it with relief. With no air conditioning in the building, it had been like wearing a portable sauna.

'What is this place?' he finally asked, his voice heavy.

'I thought you said you'd read my letter,' she said, deliberately keeping her tone breezy. She opened the cloth sack in the corner and folded the onesie into it, stuffing the wig and nose in its pockets.

However this conversation went, she would not allow it to affect her. The children were very sensitive to undercurrents of mood.

'I read what I thought was enough.'

'What did you think it was?'

'A crèche.'

'Really?'

His jaw tightened. 'You look pleased.'

'I am.' She crossed her arms and gave him a rueful smile. 'Your reaction is more forgivable if you thought this was an ordinary day care centre for ordinary kids from ordinary families.'

His lips tightened, his throat moving.

Unbelievably, she felt a pang of sorrow for him and his cynical view of her.

'Do you understand why I had to be here today? If I hadn't, the centre wouldn't have opened. It's a lifeline for their families as well as for the kids.'

'Who are these children?'

'Children who, whether by birth or accident, will never lead a normal life but who have enough awareness to *want* a normal life.'

She wished she could read his eyes and know what was happening in his brain.

'Stay for a few hours.' Reaching out, she brushed her fingers on his hand before placing them down her side. 'See what we do here and what your money is saving.'

After a beat he said, quietly, 'We'll leave when you're ready.'

Her heart lighter than it had felt in a very long time, she walked by his side back to the day room.

Lunch was in full swing so she went through to the dining room to help. As was usual, it looked as if a food war had broken out. She glanced at Raul, whose attention had been taken by a board with smiling pictures of all the staff.

'You're a volunteer?'

'Yes.'

He nodded slowly, his eyes narrowing but not in a way that made her skin go cold. This time there was no contempt in that look, only contemplation. 'What do you want me to do?'

She stared at his Armani suit and grinned. 'Help the kids eat.'

A tug on her shorts had her lowering herself automati-

cally to take Karin into her arms, whereby the little girl
immediately prodded her then covered her face in sloppy
kisses.

'Come on, let's get you fed,' she said, carrying Karin
to her own special seat at the table and opening her lunch-
box for her.

She looked to where Raul had brought over a chair to
help Ramon eat his dinner, quietly sniggering at what she
knew would happen next. Ramon, possibly the messiest
eater of them all, was eating a centre-cooked hot meal of
carbonara.

Oh, well, she thought cheerfully, Raul could afford the
dry-cleaning bill.

Once back in Barcelona, the sun setting on the horizon,
they stopped at a pizzeria for something to eat, wedging
themselves on an outside table inches from the pavement.

One thing Charley had always appreciated about Raul
was his lack of snobbery when it came to food. His tastes
were refined towards everything else but he would happily wolf down anything put in front of him. When she'd
suggested they eat here rather than somewhere fancy, he'd
shrugged his shoulders and agreed.

Fancy food was something she'd had to get used to
when they'd married, having been raised on a diet that
consisted mostly of microwave meals or baked beans on
toast. A chocolate bar or ice cream had been their usual
form of dessert.

How simple everything had been back then. Her mum
had been young and naïve but incredibly hardworking.
She'd held down two jobs for as far back as Charley could
remember but had always made sure she was home to have
dinner with her only child. Half the time she was unaware

her daughter had skived off school again and had spent the day watching music videos on the television.

Charley had never doubted her mum's love for her.

It was her father's love she'd always doubted, a thought she shoved firmly from her mind, feeling disloyal to even *think* it. Of *course* her dad loved her—he told her so every time he saw her.

She just wished she could have seen more of him but he had always been so busy, running his latest get-rich-quick scheme and being with her half-brothers. This had been completely understandable; her half-brothers had lived in the same town as him. A visit to his daughter every few months had been the most time he could spare. And he *had* visited her home on a whim once, when she'd been at school. He'd left a note for her saying he'd been there. If that didn't prove he loved her and carried her in his thoughts, what did?

And if her days skiving off school, watching music videos, had been spent hovering on the sofa by the window that had overlooked their flat's car park, and every time she'd seen a dark blue estate car pull into it her heart would accelerate with excitement that maybe he was paying her another unannounced visit…well, it was hardly his fault that he'd never made another unexpected trip, was it? Her dad hadn't known she'd been sitting there in hope, waiting for him.

'How did you get involved with the centre?' Raul asked once their order had been taken.

'I went there as a volunteer to entertain the children…'

'Yes, but *how*? Did you see an advert?'

'Kind of. I decided to do some voluntary work to pass the time while deciding what to do with my life. I've always liked children and keeping them entertained is about the only thing I've ever been good at.'

All those teenage years sitting alone in the flat in the hope her dad would eventually turn up instead of knuckling down at school had left her with nothing to show for over a decade of education. It was only after she'd left school and seen how severely limited her options were that she'd understood what she'd thrown away: her future. She'd never given the future any real thought; the present had been enough to cope with. Her mum had been so disappointed too, although she'd tried to cover it up with an understanding hug. That one hug had spurred Charley on more than any career advice she could have been given.

She might have no qualifications but she *would* make something of herself. She'd always loved kids, had danced along to enough music videos to have gained some decent rhythm, so being an entertainer at family resorts had seemed the logical thing to do.

But meeting Raul and his brilliant mind had only served to magnify her past mistakes and she'd been determined to rectify them, to make her mum's sacrifices worthwhile, to make Raul proud and to make their future children proud. She'd clutched at business ideas that had looked good on paper but held no emotional appeal. She hadn't thought it mattered. All that had mattered was proving herself a success.

All she'd proved was that she was a failure.

How could *anyone* respect her, let alone her husband and future children?

'I went to the children's hospital first to see if they needed or wanted any volunteers and through them I met one of the kids who went to the centre,' she continued, forcing brightness into her voice. 'I went along once to see if they had any need for me, fell in love with the place and ended up volunteering on a permanent basis.'

'Could they not pay you?'

'They could barely afford the staff they did have.' A whimsical smile crossed her face. 'Besides, I had the money to support myself.'

While he tried to digest all this and process the shifting sands of his opinion towards her, their pizzas were brought to their table.

'Where does the centre get its money from?'

'Are you telling me you bought the new building for us without looking through any of the financial reports I'd made?'

'There hasn't been the time.' It didn't strike him as the right time to confess he'd assumed her financial reports would be worth less than the paper they were written on. He'd fished them out of the shredding pile but was still to sit down and read them.

He had misjudged her terribly.

From the knowing look in her eyes, she knew it too.

'The parents who can afford it pay a day rate,' she said. 'But most of the funds come from donations and grants. It's enough to keep the place ticking over but not enough to build a healthy reserve.'

'Do you do much in the way of fundraising?'

'As much as we can. We'd hoped to devote more time to fundraising and awareness this year but obviously recent events put the brakes on that.'

Raul chewed in silence, thinking.

He'd spent less than five hours in the centre but that had been long enough for him to know he wanted to help.

'Why didn't you come to me?'

'I did.'

'I mean before, when you first learned the building was being sold out from under your feet.'

She dropped her gaze from his and picked up a slice of spicy pizza. 'I thought I could do it myself.'

The same way she'd always thought she could run her businesses on her own even though she didn't have the tools. In the end it had become a battle of wills between them. The more he'd tried to help, the more she'd pushed him away.

'Is that why you wanted to do it in your own name? For the glory?'

He knew the answer even as her eyes shot back up to him and her cheeks tightened in on themselves. 'No! I wanted to *help*. Poco Rio has no assets, no back-up capital. I thought I had enough money left to pay for it all. All I could think was *let's get this done*, but I had it in my head that once it was complete I would get some kind of charity established and hand it all over so Poco Rio would always be guaranteed a home.'

She put her pizza down without taking a bite and took a large sip of her lager.

She'd drunk lager on their first date. It was only after he'd brought her to Barcelona that her palate had taken an immediate preference to fine wine.

All along he'd made assumptions but if his assumption that Charley was a gold-digger had been wrong—and today had only confirmed what his senses had been trying to tell him for weeks—what else was he wrong about?

He thought of all the lengths he'd gone to throughout his childhood and adolescence in his increasingly desperate bids to impress his father, working so hard on his studies, often studying until the early hours, regularly turning down invitations that took him away from his books, determined to be the top-ranked student in his private school. He'd succeeded in that aim, leaving school with the highest grades possible and a personal recommendation from the headmaster. His father's response had been an uninterested grunt and the words, 'Let's see how you get on at MIT when you're competing against the best brains in the world.'

Had he somehow caused Charley to feel the same inadequacies his father had caused him?

Dios. No. He had loved her. He hadn't wanted to change her, just make her adapt to his life with ease so she *didn't* feel those inadequacies.

But that strange feeling of witnessing the Ghost of Wife Past whispered through him again, a hollow ache expanding through his chest.

'With my contacts and media presence, we can raise awareness and funds,' he said, before draining his own lager.

'That would be amazing.' The emotion in her eyes sparkled into joy, her cheeks widening into a smile. 'The more funds we raise, the more staff we can employ and the more kids we can take in.'

As he peppered her with more questions about the project, her animation grew.

It was an animation he'd never seen when she'd been planning her own businesses.

She looked magnificent, her green eyes swirling, her hands gesticulating.

When he suggested doing a fundraising cruise on his brand-new liner, her pizza almost flew out of her hand in her excitement.

Eventually their plates were empty, desserts consumed along with coffee to finish.

Raul checked his watch and was surprised to find they'd been sitting there for three hours. If not for the sun having set, he would have said no longer than an hour. He called for the bill then threw Charley a lazy smile before covering her hand. 'Let's go home.'

Her eyes brightened before cooling. 'Am I still expected to stick to our pact?'

'Of course. We have an agreement, *cariño*.' He leaned forward to place his cheek against hers, inhaling the scent of faded vanilla. 'Nothing has changed.'

Inside, though, he knew that *everything* had changed.

If he had any kind of decency, he would make their pact void.

They would stay together, he decided, until the renovations were complete. He would give her all the support he could to see it through to its conclusion. They would work together, just as he should have insisted in their marriage's first incarnation.

The simple truth was that he wasn't ready to say goodbye to her. Not yet.

He never had been.

A whispering voice inside him told him he never would be.

CHAPTER TEN

CHARLEY STOOD IN her dressing room, nose wrinkling as she tried to decide what to wear. If she was going to the centre she would wear something casual, which food and paints could be splattered all over. Dressing for a day in Raul's HQ required an entirely different form of dress. It required the kind of attire she'd shunned since she'd left him.

High-powered business outfits left her cold.

So far she'd mixed and matched anything suitable she could find but was quickly running out of options.

She sighed. She supposed she should take a shopping trip to stock up. Mixing and matching wouldn't see her through the four months she was supposed to be at Raul's side learning the ropes of business she'd shunned all those years ago.

Why had she shunned his advice?

Had she really been so scared that allowing him to help would give him undeniable proof of her stupidity? The sad answer to that was yes. She had been scared. She hadn't wanted to give him evidence that she was less than perfect.

She'd been honest about her past and lack of education but had tried to romanticise it, to insist she had the know-how and savvy to build her own business. She'd tried to convince herself as much as him, starting her businesses with bags of enthusiasm. But she'd been faking it.

The sad fact, one she'd never been able to bring herself to admit, was that business left her as cold as the high-powered suits she'd worn. Working at Poco Rio made her feel warm.

Hearing movement in the bedroom, she turned and found Raul with a pile of papers in his arms. He'd risen early, long before she'd hauled herself out of bed.

He put the papers on her dressing table and handed the top sheet to her. 'Here's a list of my schedule for the next month. The dates highlighted are when I won't need the helicopter. You're welcome to use it on those dates to get to and from Valencia.'

She eyed him warily. She'd thought during their meal at the pizzeria last night that they were reaching an understanding, that his time at the centre had softened his attitude towards her. He'd been quick to put her straight on that.

Nothing has changed, he'd said.

And while their lovemaking when they'd returned home had been long and tender, that counted for nothing. Raul was nothing if not a generous lover. Even when he hated her.

'Are you saying I can work at the centre?'

'Yes.'

'I thought I was supposed to be glued to your hip?'

A glimmer of a smile curled on his lips. 'I would much rather have you glued to a different part of my anatomy.'

She couldn't help the burst of laughter that escaped and she almost responded with, 'So would I.' Almost.

As he'd said only the evening before, nothing had changed. He hadn't entirely reclaimed his humanity, not when he still had her in his bed as a form of punishment.

'I've been on the phone to Pierre Binoche,' he said, referring to the interior designer he used for his hotels and cruise liners, 'and have arranged a meeting with him at the end of the month at the new building. I assume you will want to be there?'

'Pierre's going to do the interior design?' she asked in amazement. 'That's incredibly good of you but, really, it's not necessary. Once all the renovations are done, all we'll need to do is give the place a lick of paint.'

'Pierre won't be discussing colour charts; he'll be looking to create the right mood for the centre. He'll take your lead, *cariño*.'

'Really?'

'You know the brief better than anyone. Think of it as PR. His name will help in the awareness drive we're going for.'

'There is that,' she conceded. This, on top of the fund-raising cruise trip, would raise so much awareness and funds for the children she felt like pinching herself to make sure it wasn't all a dream.

A thought crossed her mind. 'When at the end of the month are we meeting him?'

'The last Wednesday.'

'Oh.'

'Why?'

'The last Wednesday of August is La Tomatina. We're planning on taking some of the kids to it.'

'You're taking the children to a *tomato fight*?'

From the look on his face she might have said they were taking the children to watch bareknuckle boxing.

'Just to watch. We took five of them last year and they loved it. We sat on a roof terrace with a box of tomatoes to throw at the crowd.' La Tomatina was an annual festival in the Valencian town of Buñol.

He eyed her thoughtfully. 'Have you already got your name down to go?'

'Yes, but don't worry, I wasn't planning on stealing your helicopter again to get there.'

'You wouldn't have had any luck if you did—my pilots now know not to take you anywhere without my express permission.'

Only Raul could give with one hand and take with the other, one minute sounding human and reasonable, the next reminding her of her current position in his life. The difference now was that he said it with good humour rather than the horrid cold tone she'd hated so much. It made her hope he was thawing towards her.

She grinned mischievously. 'I wasn't going to steal your helicopter. I was going to steal your Bugatti.'

'I am going to assume you're joking or my blood pressure might combust.'

'You should come with us,' she said, speaking on impulse.

'I think not,' he said drily.

'Why not? Worried you might get your clothes dirty?'

'No.' He shook his head.

'Then why not?' Her eyes were on him, peering intently. 'Is it not becoming for a man of your standing to have a tomato fight?'

'You know perfectly well it isn't.' Raul couldn't think of anything more abhorrent than pictures of himself covered in gunk surfacing in the press and on the Internet.

'Go in disguise.'

'Charlotte, I'm not going to take a whole day off work to watch a lot of people throw tomatoes at each other.'

'Don't be such a snob. It's fun.'

'I'm not a snob.'

'Not consciously,' she conceded.

Her phone vibrated loudly. She read the message and sighed, the smile leaving her face.

Raul knew before she said anything that it was her father.

'Dad can't make it.'

He kept his features neutral. 'Why?'

There was that defensive look he recognised. 'He has a business meeting.'

'On a Saturday?'

'*You* have business meetings on Saturdays.'

'I run a multibillion-euro company. Your father is currently jobless.'

'Well, this is something to do with him finding a new job. You should be pleased he's trying to find one.'

'I am.' Raul's issue was that he simply didn't believe it. Graham had most likely found himself a date and concocted a story for his daughter's benefit rather than admitting the truth. The only good thing was that he'd had the decency to cancel in advance rather than at the last minute as he had done on numerous occasions.

The problem was, Charley didn't want to hear it.

Shaking his head, he strolled back to her dresser and picked up the rest of the papers. 'While you were sleeping, I also had the chance to look through the financial report you produced.'

'And?'

A pang shot through Raul's chest to see trepidation immediately fill her eyes.

'You did a good job.'

The trepidation was pushed out by a ray of beaming light. 'Really?'

Pulling her into his arms, he kissed her lightly and murmured, 'Really.'

He'd been astounded at how good a job she had done.

All throughout their marriage he'd believed in her innate abilities, had known she needed to harness them and focus to achieve something substantial. And now he'd been proved right.

But *she* hadn't believed it.

Why had he not recognised before that his wife had no confidence in herself?

She'd put on a good front, that was for certain. But they'd been married. How had he not seen her insecurities?

'Come on,' he said, giving her one last kiss before stepping back. 'Get dressed—I've got a meeting in half an hour.'

Before leaving the room, he turned back to her. 'Don't feel you have to dress up for the office any more. You're coming with me as my sex toy, remember?'

His heart lightened to see the grin spread across her face. 'Shall I dress as a dominatrix?'

'Now that I would *love* to see.'

Her cackle of laughter followed him out of the room.

'You've hardly stopped for the past month,' Raul said. 'Take the day off—go and see Marta.'

'Are you sure?'

'Yes.' His voice dropped. 'Unless you want to come here and take me in my office.'

Even with Raul a mile away, just the suggestive sound of his voice whispering down the phone set a frisson of heat through her.

'I'll see you when you get home,' she said firmly. 'Goodbye.'

Swiping her phone to end the call, she padded over to the window and looked out at the lashing rain and palm trees swaying in the growing wind.

It was the height of summer and Barcelona was under a deluge of water.

She was supposed to be working at the centre but the

circling storm had forced the pilot to ground the helicopter. She'd been on the verge of jumping in one of Raul's cars and driving the three-hour journey there when Seve had called, insisting he had it covered and forbidding her to go in. She could only hope the weather cleared by Wednesday. She and Raul were meeting Pierre first thing, then Charley would head over to the current centre as part of the team taking the children to La Tomatina.

But today, for once, her time was her own.

A bath. That was what she needed.

It had been ages since she'd last had a long soak.

Filling the bath until it was a steamy mass of foamy water, she climbed in and lay back, closing her eyes, happy to listen to the heavy thud of rain.

When had she last felt so content?

The past few weeks had passed in a blur. She'd travelled with Raul to St Lucia to see the development of a new hotel complex, to Madrid where the headquarters of his air fleet was located, dined out with business colleagues and friends, and still managed to work a couple of days a week at the centre.

It was amazing how different everything felt. Before, when she'd travelled with him and witnessed his burgeoning empire, her inadequacies had felt strong enough to eat her whole. So she'd stopped accompanying him, using the excuse of her own businesses to keep her rooted in Barcelona. The side effect had been the jealousy that had gripped her on their nights apart, the fear of him meeting someone more suitable that had plagued her.

Now, her inadequacies didn't matter. Her imperfections didn't matter. She and Raul were together for a strict time period. This wasn't permanent and, as a result, she no longer had to put on the pretence of being perfect. If he was concerned that she was less than perfect, he wasn't saying, and, really, why would he? Come November, they would go their separate ways. They would divorce and he could then find himself the perfect wife he needed.

A lance of pain shot through her chest as she thought of him with another woman on his arm. She sucked in her breath, holding it tightly, waiting for the feeling to pass as it always did, although it seemed to be taking longer and longer for it to pass as the days went by.

She would *not* make the same mistakes as she had before.

Mind-blowing sex did not equate to love. That was what had got her into trouble in the first place, mistaking the lust she'd felt for him for love, then, when love truly had come, it had been too late and she'd been trapped. Worse, she'd become a stranger to herself.

But this time she knew better.

This time...

Unless you want to come here and take me in my office...

She'd told herself hell would freeze over before she made the first move. As if she would give herself willingly to the man who'd blackmailed her back into his bed.

And yet...

There would be no consequences if she walked away. Raul would never back out of the centre, not now. She'd known that since he'd turned up there and been pulled into the magic of the place.

And Raul knew it too.

She could walk away and there wasn't a thing he could do or threaten her with to make her stay. Something told her that even if there were, he wouldn't use it.

For over a month she'd been telling herself that she stayed because they'd made a deal, as hateful as it had initially been.

Her eyes opened with a snap as the truth hit her.

She'd stayed because she wanted to.

Raul had done a terrible thing blackmailing her back into his bed. A *terrible* thing. He'd believed—possibly still believed—awful things about her that she could never disprove without a lie detector but over the past month he'd treated her with something he'd never shown her in all the years of their marriage. Respect.

She hadn't even known the respect had been missing until she'd found it.

Adrenaline coursed through her, her heart hammering as powerfully as the rain pouring like sheets against the window, her mind a train wreck of careering tracks.

Could their marriage work…?

No, it would be no good to think that way. Things had started well when they'd first met, when it had been all about the lust holding them together, before he'd dropped to one knee and pulled out the enormous diamond ring now locked securely away.

Their time limit meant this could be the fling their relationship should have been, the fling that should have ended with the summer and remained a beautiful memory.

A peace settled on her as she came to terms with the fact that she was no longer a hostage against her will but a full participant. Did she really want to waste the next few months, holding a part of herself back from him out of a sense of outrage that served nothing?

She lay back again and allowed her mind to drift away, images of their lovemaking filling her senses. If she concentrated really hard, she could feel the weight of his body upon her, the flicker of his tongue…

Suddenly she sat back up, sloshing water over the sides of the bath in her haste, as a deliciously naughty thought came into her head.

'Unless you want to come here and take me in my office...' Raul had said.

If she was going to be a full participant in this, then it was time to let Raul know, to put their relationship on the equal footing it deserved.

And she knew *just* the way.

Raul sipped at his water, forcing himself to concentrate on the letter he was dictating straight into his laptop for his PA and trying not to think of Charley at home alone, trying to rid himself of thoughts of finishing early to return to her.

The phone on his desk buzzed.

He paused mid-sentence and frowned down at it. His executive team knew he was dictating and not to disturb him.

He pressed the offending buzzer and spoke into it. 'Is there a problem?'

'Your wife is here,' came the voice of Ava. 'She says it's important she speak to you.'

Immediately his mind went into overdrive, imagining all the things that could have driven her here, something icy clutching at his heart. This could not be anything good.

'Let her in.'

The past month, things had been good between them. Better than he'd dreamed they could be, even when they'd first exchanged their vows and their whole future had been a blank canvas waiting for them to paint with glorious colour.

Too good. Highs were always followed by lows.

The door opened and Charley stepped in, dressed for the awful weather in a long black trench coat.

He rose from his seat. 'Whatever's the matter?'

A serene smile on her face, she closed the door quietly behind her.

'Sit down,' she said softly.

Raul would be the first to admit that confusion rarely entered his vocabulary, but right then... 'What?'

Her hands went to the belt of her trench coat.

'I said...' her voice was quiet but knowing as she tugged the belt loose '...sit...' her hands went to the lapels and pulled them apart '...down.'

Under her coat she was as naked as the day she'd been born.

Shrugging it off, she sashayed towards him in high black heels, her breasts moving with the motion, her nipples drawing his attention.

He blinked, suddenly certain he'd fallen asleep at his desk.

She placed a hand to his chest and pushed him back onto his chair, the height of her heels lifting her so his face was almost level with the top of her thighs.

The effect on him was instantaneous.

Her smile had lost its serenity, had become something heavy and sensual.

Placing a hand on his shoulder, she hooked a leg over his lap to straddle him, keeping her shoes on the ground so she was elevated over him. The only part of her touching him was the hand on his shoulder and her inner thighs. Not a single inch of her touched his bare skin yet he felt scorched by her touch.

Her hand slipped round his neck and she leaned forward to breathe into his ear. 'I thought I would take you up on your offer.'

With the heavy weight of her breasts pressed against his chest and her warm scent clinging to her like a cloud, coherent thoughts were a world away.

'Which offer?'

She moved her lips across his cheek until she reached

his mouth while tracing a hand over his shirt-clad chest and down to the belt of his trousers.

'To take you in your office.'

Her mouth didn't move from his as she worked at his belt then unzipped him, with just a whisper of her lips touching him. He placed a hand on her waist, the warmth and softness of her skin deepening the burn in his loins.

He didn't think he'd ever been aroused so quickly and so deeply as he felt right now or ever been as aware of the sound of his blood pumping.

A sudden urgency rippled through him and he reached down to help tug his opened trousers and boxers down enough to free him. Immediately she took hold of him.

He inhaled deeply to stop the groan that wanted to escape.

Her breaths coming out in shallow pants, she guided him to her opening, and sank down on him.

This time his groan could not be held at bay and as his mouth parted she moaned into him, the sound of their pleasure muffled.

She broke away from his mouth and raised herself, placing her hands on his shoulders to steady herself, then sank back down.

With a hand on her back and the other on her hip, Raul began to move with her, bucking upwards to meet her downward thrusts, unable to tear his gaze from her eyes.

They were filled with wonder and ecstasy and it was all directed at him.

But the urgency was there too, for both of them, the movements quickening, pressing closer and closer together until he had her crushed against him and her mouth and tongue were twined with his.

He felt her tighten around him and fought to hold on,

right until she sank one final time and shuddered, clinging to him.

And then it was time for his release.

It ripped through him, blinding him with its savage
force, his whole body shuddering as he fought for every
last drop of the pleasure consuming him.

He had no idea how long they sat there afterwards,
fused together, faces buried in each other's necks, the only
sound their ragged breathing.

It was only when she raised her face to kiss him that
some form of sanity came back to him.

'I need to use your bathroom,' she murmured, climb-
ing off him. She grinned, then sashayed on obviously un-
steady feet to his adjoining restroom.

Alone, he blew out a burst of warm air and got to his
feet, sorting out his clothes, his dazed brain slowly clearing.

That had to count as the most unexpected and erotic
experience of his life.

In no time at all, Charley slipped back into the office
and scooped her coat from the floor.

She met Raul's eye and grinned again as she slipped
her arms into the sleeves and tightened the belt around
her waist.

Stepping back over to him, she slid her arms around his
neck and reached up to kiss him. She made to leave but he
caught her wrist and pulled her back to him, cupping her
cheeks to give her one final, deep, passionate kiss.

The serene smile lighting her face, Charley left his office as silently as she'd come.

Raul flopped back onto his chair and rubbed his eyes.

Had that really happened?

In all the years of their marriage, Charley had never
done anything like this. Not once. The closest had been

her dressing up for him in sexy lingerie and seducing him in their bedroom.

He felt a twitch in his loins as he saw again her opening that long coat to reveal her shimmering nakedness.

Dios.

She'd been so ready for him.

Dios.

Dragging a hand through his hair, he tried to force his concentration back on the work before him but knew he was fighting a losing battle.

She'd be back home soon.

He felt the twitch in his loins again and gritted his teeth.

Would she get dressed or would she stay naked?

He punched the buzzer of his phone. 'Get me a coffee,' he ordered, forgetting his usual pleasantries. 'And make it a strong one.'

Only through ruthless control did he manage to get any more work done that day. His libido never quite returned to dormancy, a dull ache there that he studiously ignored, determined to get his work complete as quickly as possible so he could return home to his wife waiting there for him. Not just waiting for him but openly wanting him.

His heart felt so full and weighty he could feel it pressing against his chest.

CHAPTER ELEVEN

Raul fastened his seat belt wondering what exactly he'd agreed to.

They'd met Pierre at the new centre, along with Vittore and Pablo, the project manager. Seve had also joined them, enthusing about all the renovation work being undertaken.

Charley had been in her element, eyes shining, her happiness as bright as the sun blazing in the sky.

The storm that had covered great swathes of Spain over the past few days had lifted. His spirits had turned with it.

'It would be better if I drove,' he said, watching as she adjusted the driver's seat. He'd never been a passenger with his wife behind the wheel.

'You're not insured,' Charley said blithely, switching the engine on.

'It will take one minute to get me on the insurance.'

'I'm driving.' And with that, she put the minibus into reverse and they were on their way, ambling towards the town of Buñol.

Five of the children were strapped in the back with two of the other workers and another volunteer, all the children in a heightened state of excitement. From what Charley had said, they displayed the same level of enthusiasm towards trips to the local swimming baths and the supermarket.

The plan had been for him to drive Charley to the centre

then head back to Barcelona, but then she'd turned those gorgeous green eyes on him and said, 'Come with us.'

He still didn't understand why he hadn't just refused as he had when she'd first suggested it. Said *No, I've far too much work to do to spend time watching a bunch of people throw tomatoes at each other.*

Most likely it was curiosity, to see for himself the event regarded as the world's biggest food fight.

It wasn't, he assured himself, because being away from Charley was becoming a physical pain.

There was no doubt though that their relationship had shifted dramatically since her seduction in his office. The last of her reserve towards him had vanished.

When they made love now nothing was held back. She laughed easily and walked as if she had springs implanted in her shoes.

She was happy. Being with *him* made her happy.

Being with her was like being with the woman he'd first fallen in love with...

When they arrived at the tiny hotel that overlooked Plaza del Pueblo, where most of the action would be taking place, they were greeted by the manager who led them straight up to the small roof terrace. From what Raul could see, their spot was one of the only ones that allowed spectators to actually see what was unfolding.

And what a sight it was. Tens of thousands of men and women were crammed in the plaza and the surrounding narrow streets, haulage trucks filled with crate upon crate of ripe tomatoes placed strategically alongside water cannons. Many of the shop fronts and homes had been protected with huge plastic sheets. Scores of mostly young men were attempting to shimmy their way up a two-storey pole with what looked like a hock of ham at the top, but he guessed it must be greased for the men got no further than a couple of feet before sliding back down on top of each other, only to immediately try again.

Chairs had been laid out for them; the terrace was safe enough for the kids to jump up and down with the excitement of it all.

Never in his wildest dreams had Raul imagined he would take a day off work to watch a tomato fight, and he imagined the look on his father's face if he were to learn what his son had done. The disapproval would be as clear as the juice of the ripe tomatoes.

'Next year I'm going to try and spend the week here and join in with the whole festival,' Charley said, shouting over the chants of *'Olé, olé, olé, olé!'* bellowing from the crowd. Her cheeks were flushed with excitement. Karin climbed onto her lap and she automatically put her arm around her waist to secure her. 'I bet you'd love it too.'

Before he could respond, the roar of the water cannons signalled the start of the fight.

Carnage ensued, joyous, messy, glorious carnage.

Charley and the kids were in fits of laughter watching overripe tomatoes being thrown and squelched in all directions, the streets and the people that filled them soon a river of red juice.

He could hardly credit that he, Raul Cazorla, a man who enjoyed the finest of all the world had to offer, was enjoying something so…unrefined.

When he'd been growing up, his mother would have rather gone without her weekly pedicure than allow her children to attend something so messy and unbecoming. The Cazorlas had an image they protected fiercely; they were seen at the right places in the right clothes. The annual tomato fight at Buñol, preceded by a week-long festival, would most certainly have fallen onto the 'unbecoming for a Cazorla' list.

Something wet and squelchy slapped into his back. Turning his head, he saw that one of the children had thrown a tomato at him and was laughing so hard tears were falling down his face.

He saw the box of tomatoes, feet away from him, right at the moment Charley placed Karin on her seat and ran for it, grabbing a couple of tomatoes. Grinning widely, she squished them in her hands, then lobbed them at him.

He gazed down at what seconds before had been an immaculately pressed white silk shirt and was now dripping in juice and pips.

The others had got in on the act, except for Karin, who was clapping her hands, not knowing what was happening but reacting to the sounds of delight ringing out.

Charley dipped back into the box, her eyes sending out a clear challenge.

Raul never turned down a challenge.

Charley couldn't remember ever having experienced such a magical day.

By the time the tomato fight had finished, they'd been as red as the people in the streets. The hotel manager had appeared with a hose to wash them all down. They'd returned to the centre wet and exhausted but happy.

'You looked like you enjoyed yourself today,' she said as they left the car park. It had surprised and delighted her how Raul had really got into the spirit of things on that little terrace, accepting the splatters of tomatoes from the children with good humour and retaliating with the gentlest of throws. His retaliation of her own throws at him had been markedly different; at one point he'd pinned her arms behind her back and encouraged the kids to use her as a target before squishing one right under her T-shirt.

She was certain there were tomato pips stuck in the wiring of her bra.

He nodded musingly, bringing the car to a stop at a junction. 'It was fun.'

'Wasn't it? Saying that, my arms are killing me after all that tomato throwing.' She eyed him suggestively. 'I think I need a good massage.'

His hand drifted over to her thigh and gently squeezed. 'I'm sure I can think of a good masseur.'

'I'm sure you can.'

With his hand resting on her thigh, she rested her head against the window and closed her eyes with a contented sigh. 'Do you know how the ticket sales for the fundraiser are going?' she asked.

Raul had got a team of his people to organise the fundraiser, for which they were charging obscenely rich people obscenely high ticket prices. Charley was fully involved in the practicalities but not with the ticket sales.

She heard the clicking of his tongue on the roof of his mouth. 'I was waiting for the right moment to share this with you,' he said in a chiding voice.

'Oh, just tell me!'

'We've sold out.'

'No way!' If the traffic hadn't chosen that moment to start moving again, she would have thrown herself at him. 'That's amazing.'

'I have a good team.'

She hugged her arms, doing the maths in her head. 'Ticket sales alone will guarantee everyone's salary is paid for the next two years.'

'By the time the fundraiser is over, you'll be able to guarantee salaries for the next decade.' He laughed.

That made her sit up. 'Wow. Just think, with those kinds of funds we'll be able to afford more staff and start taking teenagers in. The builders are dividing the building into two separate parts so there can be adolescent quarters, but we never thought we'd be able to start taking them this soon.'

'You can start paying yourself a salary too,' he said lightly.

'I don't know about that.' She shook her head. 'It doesn't sit right. I've got enough money left that, if I'm careful, should last me a long while yet.'

'You have two hundred thousand euros, which you were prepared to give to the new centre, not loan. If you'd been successful in raising the rest of the money by other means, you would have been left penniless.'

'How do you…? Oh, yes, you read my finance report.' She'd listed on it how much of her own money she'd intended to contribute to the project, which had basically been everything in her account and her jewellery, all of which she'd sold with the exception of her wedding and engagement rings. As sentimental as she'd known it to be, she hadn't been able to bring herself to part with them.

'So you are intending to stay at the centre?'

'What else can I do?'

'You can start by drawing a salary. God knows, you work hard enough.'

'Hardly. I just joke around and make the kids laugh.' That was about all she was good for, she thought, her mood suddenly darkening.

'You do a lot more than that.'

She shrugged.

'Charlotte, if it wasn't for you, the children wouldn't have a new centre to look forward to and the staff would be job-hunting as we speak.'

'If it wasn't for *you*, you mean.' While she had spent two months beating at doors to get the funding, putting an immediate freeze on personal spending other than on the bare necessities, selling anything of value, boiling her brain over design plans and finance reports, Raul had swept in and taken care of everything as easily as if he were taking a shower.

He drove them through the gate to the hangar. The Cazorla helicopter sat ahead of them, gleaming in the early evening sun. 'You did all the hard work. The renovations are being done according to your plans. Vittore has adapted them a little but it's still your work. Take the credit for it. You've earned it.'

'Twaddle. I didn't do anything that anyone else couldn't have done.'

He banged his fist on the steering wheel, making her jump.

'When,' he said tightly, 'are you going to stop putting yourself down?'

'I'm not putting myself down,' she protested. 'I'm just saying that anyone else in my position would have done the same.'

He pulled the car to a stop and gazed at her with an intensity that sent a not unpleasant shiver running up her spine.

'No,' he said slowly. 'I don't think many people in your position would have done the same.'

She swallowed, staring at him, trying to read what lay behind the intensity.

'Sometimes, Señora Cazorla, I look at you and I remember exactly why I fell in love with you.'

A loud buzzing played in her ears. Her throat ran so dry no amount of swallowing could moisten it.

She cleared her suddenly arid throat. 'Your pilot's waiting for us.'

His gaze held a moment longer before he smiled and shook his head.

* * *

'More wine?'

Charley blinked. She'd been a thousand miles away.

She breathed deeply and fixed a smile to her face. 'Go on, then. We might as well order our food too.' They'd been in the restaurant for an hour and still there was no sign of her dad. Neither was he answering his phone.

'Are you sure?'

She gazed back at the menu open on her lap. She didn't want to look at Raul or the sympathy radiating from him.

He was only an hour late. For her dad, that was nothing. As a kid she'd often spent whole days waiting for him to arrive.

'Definitely. The minute we order is the minute he'll arrive,' she said brightly. 'You wait, he'll be here any second.'

'Of course he will,' Raul agreed with eyes that said he thought the total opposite.

She snatched up her glass and downed the last of the red liquid. Forget bouquets of blackcurrant and cinnamon and whatever else it was reputed to have, the only attribute she cared for was its anaesthetic quality.

She was an adult now, she reminded herself, and had long ago accepted her dad for who he was: a man who had certain reliability issues.

Yet waiting for him as an adult still made her feel like the little girl who would wait for hours for his car to pull into the car park, and the adolescent who would skive off school for fear of missing out on an unexpected visit from him.

He would be here.

They ordered their dishes and more drinks were brought over.

Her phone vibrated.

She knew what it would say before she opened it.

'Has something come up?' Raul asked carefully, while she read her dad's brief message. He didn't need to be psychic either.

She forced a cheerful smile to her face and nodded. 'There's something wrong with his car—it's making strange noises. He doesn't think it's safe to continue the drive.'

She'd *known* she should have travelled to him and would have done if she hadn't been spending the day at Poco Rio. When she was the one to make the effort there was less chance of some emergency cropping up at the last minute.

But…since her dad had moved to the Costa Dorado, he hadn't made the effort to visit her once. The intention had been there though, she reminded herself. They'd made plenty of dates for him to come to her. She'd even bought him a car so he could get around and not be stuck in his beachside home.

She should have arranged to meet him in Barcelona, not here in Valencia. Barcelona was much closer to him.

'That's a shame,' Raul said.

'There'll be another time.'

Another time for him to stand her up.

It had been bad enough worrying that Raul was going to be late for the meal too. He'd travelled to Brazil on Wednesday, only arriving back that afternoon. Two nights of fret and worry.

Sometimes, when she let her mind wander too far, she heard his words echo in her head. *'Sometimes, Señora Cazorla, I look at you and I remember exactly why I fell in love with you.'*

She'd laughed it off but under the bonhomie she'd turned into a wreck. His words had terrified her.

If he'd loved her so much then why had he given up on her so easily? Two years of silence had said it all.

He'd made her into the perfect Cazorla wife but as soon as she'd denied him what he wanted, a child, he'd given up on her.

Just as her father only wanted her when he needed money. Charley was disposable.

Nothing similar had been mentioned in the subsequent weeks but those words had stayed with her.

Then he'd gone off to Brazil, the land of beautiful women, leaving her alone for the first time since they'd got back together—got back together *temporarily*, she reminded herself—and found herself alone in *his* huge bed with a brain that refused to switch off.

They were only temporary, her brain had screamed. In less than a couple of months they would head their separate ways.

Oh, why had he said it? Why had he mentioned the L word?

He hadn't said he loved her now. Just that he'd loved her then.

But he didn't love you then. If he had he would never have tried to change you.

In defiance, she'd rolled over to the middle of the bed.

Come the morning and after a few hours of broken sleep, she'd been back on her own side with his pillow in her arms. She'd had to stop those same arms throwing themselves around him when he'd arrived at Poco Rio late that afternoon, as they were clearing up after a long day. She'd wanted to hug him even harder when he'd taken her briefly to the new centre so she could see how all the renovations were going.

'Oh, stop pretending to be nice about it,' she snapped now, suddenly and unbelievably on the brink of tears. 'We both know my dad couldn't give a stuff about me.'

To her horror, she only noticed her hands were shaking when Raul took one of them in his own.

'Do you know my dad's the only person not happy that we're back together?' she said, speaking the words before she could call them back. 'He'll want to meet up when he knows you're out of the picture. Either then or if he runs out of money before our time's up.'

He didn't answer, his blue eyes holding hers, sympathy and not a little anger in them.

Raul had got the measure of her dad right from the start.

She jerked her hand out of his grasp, picked up her re-filled glass and held it aloft. 'Happy birthday to me, eh?'

'Charlotte…'

'Don't worry about it,' she dismissed, putting her glass back down. 'This isn't the first of my birthdays he's missed and I'm sure it won't be the last.'

Twenty-six birthdays and her dad had only made two of them.

'Charlotte,' he repeated, speaking quietly, 'this isn't your fault.'

She attempted a smile, now really scared that she would cry. 'I know.'

At least, it wasn't her fault she'd been born a woman. She'd always known that if she'd been born with male genitals her father would have wanted to spend more time with her, just as he did with her half-brothers. Deep down she'd always known it, just never acknowledged the painful truth.

She was a mere woman. Disposable.

A waitress arrived at their table with their first course.

Charley stabbed a piece of chorizo with her fork. Before she could pop it in her mouth, more unbidden words spilled out. 'I've never mattered to him. I look back on my childhood and all I can clearly remember is the waiting. I used to get so excited when I knew he was coming over. Half the time he'd be late—at the very least an hour—the other half he wouldn't turn up at all. When he did bother, he'd always have a great big present for me that cost the earth, then tell my mum he didn't have the money to buy me a new pair of school shoes.'

She took a breath and another sip of wine, wondering why she was rehashing a tale Raul was already familiar with. But there was one story she'd never shared...

'I have never spent a single Christmas with him,' she said, keeping her eyes on her glass of wine, 'and I only got invited to celebrate one of his birthdays—his fortieth. I was about nine, I think, and Mum and I went together. I remember being really excited about meeting my two half-brothers. Dad had told me *all* about them. I knew he lived close to them and saw them a lot.'

Now she dared look at Raul. 'They didn't know who I was.'

'I suppose that's understandable, seeing as they'd never met you.'

'No—I mean they didn't know *of* me. My dad had never told them they had a sister.'

Raul tried to keep his features composed, not to let Charley see the anger her words were provoking in him.

He had little doubt that if her father should walk into the restaurant at that moment he would connect his fist to his face with all the force in his possession. How that man had the nerve to call himself a father...

How Charley had managed to grow up into the warm, compassionate woman she was today stumped him too.

'Can we go home?' she asked. 'I've got a headache.'

She did look pale.

He called for the bill and discreetly told the waitress to cancel the cake waiting in the kitchen that was to have been brought out when their meal had finished. Getting to his feet, he felt in his pocket for the square box. He would give Charley her present when they got home, after a relaxing massage and a bottle of champagne. He would spoil her rotten and make this a birthday to remember for all the right reasons.

But first he had to get them home.

CHAPTER TWELVE

THE STREETS SURROUNDING the restaurant were gridlocked, the pavements packed with people spilling out of the nearby theatre, Teatro Olympia.

Wedging them comfortably in the stream of the traffic, Raul put the car in neutral and rested his head back.

His chest filled to see Charley gaze out of the passenger window, chewing her little finger, her silent pain pulling at him, making him want to hold her tight and stroke all the heartache away.

'How much money have you given him over the past few years?' he asked quietly.

She raised a shoulder but didn't look at him. 'I didn't keep track. A quarter of a million in all, I think.'

'On top of the house?'

A sharp nod.

He sighed, feeling even more strongly for her.

A cacophony of beeping cars broke through the silence and, with a start, he realised they were beeping at him.

He put the car into gear and pressed gently on the accelerator. 'What did you do with the rest of the money?'

'What do you think I did with it?' she asked, turning her head to look at him, a curious expression on her face.

'I don't know.' Every single one of his assumptions about her had been wrong, that much he did know. 'I don't think you spent it all on yourself.'

'I bought some houses.'

'You went into property?'

She let out a muted bark of laughter. '*No.* I didn't *go into* property. I bought houses—one for my mum...'

'*I* bought your mum a house,' he interjected. Unlike Charley's father, who he wouldn't spit on if he were on fire, her mum he did like and he'd been happy to buy her a decent place to live. He'd bought it as a Christmas present for her, keeping it a surprise from both her *and* Charley.

He knew Charley's mood would be lighter if her mum could have been here to celebrate her birthday too, but Charley's grandmother had had a hip replacement the week before and Paula was staying with her.

'That was in England. I bought her a holiday home here in Valencia so she could visit whenever she wanted and have a place to stay; my home is a little cramped for two. Also,' she added as an afterthought, 'I thought it unfair my dad was getting a Spanish home when she couldn't have the same.'

He grinned, liking her way of thinking.

'Who else did you buy houses for?'

'My half-brothers and—'

'Why on earth did you buy them homes?' Raul had never met her half-brothers and had no wish to. Like her father, they only bothered with her when they wanted some money. 'Let me make an educated guess—your dad told them we'd separated and that you had some money in your own right so they took the opportunity to get in touch and played you with a good sob story?'

'Wrong.' She scowled at him. 'I bought them because I wanted to. They might keep their distance but they're the only siblings I've got.'

'Did you buy them cars too?'

She nodded.

'Who else?' he asked, with a sigh. There was no point in arguing about the wrongs or rights of it. There was truth in the saying that blood was thicker than water. Charley had been right in her criticisms of his own family but that hadn't stopped them needling him like barbs in his skin.

'My grandparents and my auntie Beverley.'

'Is that it?'

'Isn't that enough?'

She wasn't being facetious. Her question was genuine.

'Enough? Charlotte, that money was for *you*.'

'And I did spend some of it on me. I wasn't completely selfless, you know. I bought myself my villa and a car, and until recently I've been taking monthly visits to the hairdresser. They all needed homes of their own far more than I needed another exotic holiday.'

'Why didn't you tell me you wanted to buy your family houses?'

'I couldn't have asked you to do that,' she said, clearly horrified at the idea.

'Why not? We were married.' He didn't know what was worse: knowing he'd thought the worst about her or learning that she hadn't felt secure enough in their marriage to think she could ask him for anything.

He'd thought he'd given her everything she'd wanted and needed.

Suddenly it hit him with force, like a punch to his solar plexus. It had *all* been a lie.

'You never opened up to me at all, did you?'

She must have caught something in his tone because her eyes became wary. 'What do you mean?'

'In the whole of our marriage you never trusted me, did you?'

'I did trust you. I told you before I knew you wouldn't cheat on me…'

'That is *not* trust!' A fraction too late, he saw the flashing brake lights of the car in front and slammed his foot down, missing the car in front by inches. 'You trusted me not to cheat but you didn't trust me with what was going on in your head.' He took in a breath. 'I loved you but you were never honest about anything, were you? You started all those businesses without having any real interest in any of them but didn't have the guts to tell me. If you'd had an ounce of the passion for them that you have for the centre, they would have succeeded.'

He took in her red checked silk top, black crepe trousers and short black heels, a classy combination that, with her blonde hair twisted in a simple knot, looked stunning on her but was markedly different from the clothes she used to wear.

'You even wear different clothes.' He shook his head and breathed deeply, struggling to comprehend.

Dios. Even her clothing had been a lie.

'What did I do that was so bad you couldn't trust me with the truth about yourself or your feelings? Did I ever mistreat you in any way?'

'Of course you never mistreated me...'

'Then *what*? I loved you.'

Her eyes became pincers. 'If you loved me as much as you say you did, then why did you try to change me?'

'I didn't try to change you.'

'Well, that's what it felt like,' she said, a tremor carrying in her voice. She rubbed her forehead. 'Before we'd even exchanged our vows you'd thrown tutors at me to teach me elocution and all that other stuff. You got your sister to take me shopping to all the best places, you hired me my own personal trainer and dietician... The only reason you went to all that effort was because I wasn't good enough for you and your perfect family as I was.'

'For the last time, I was trying to help you fit in.'

'And why was that? It was because I *didn't* fit in.'

He slammed his fist on the steering wheel. 'I was trying to protect you!'

Astonishment crossed her features. 'Protect me from what?'

'From my world and the people who live in it. I didn't want you in social situations where you felt intimidated or unable to hold your own.'

Silence rang out between them, the only sound their ragged breaths and the pounding in his head.

'From now on, no more lies,' he said when he felt more in control of himself.

'They weren't deliberate lies,' she whispered. 'I was just so desperate to fit in and make you proud. I was terrified you would meet someone more suitable and drop me like a hot rock.'

'That would never have happened. When I married you it was for ever, not until someone better came along.'

'But I didn't believe it—how could I when I spent my whole life believing I was so insignificant my own father only wanted to see me when he had nothing better to do? That I wasn't good enough to even deserve a mention to his other family?' She blew air out of her mouth and rested her head back to gaze at the roof of the car. 'How can you understand what that feels like when everything you touch turns into gold?'

He swallowed, her words like claws gripping at his skin.

Not understand how she'd felt? The boy who'd grown up having every tiny mistake and digression magnified under his father's totalitarian disapproval?

'I know what it looks like on the surface but my life hasn't been totally charmed. I know what it's like to feel useless and inferior.'

'When have *you* ever felt inferior?' she asked, twisting to face him, her eyes wide.

'My father...' He cut his words off and attempted to gather his thoughts. If he was demanding honesty from her, then it was only right he give it in return, however hard it was to get the words out. Without honesty, they had no future. 'I could never please him. Nothing I did was ever good enough.'

Her brows drew together.

'He was a cold, cruel man—a hard taskmaster. He had exacting standards he expected me to live up to and if I failed in any aspect then he made his displeasure known. I don't remember doing anything that pleased him or raised a smile to his face. If he felt any affection for me he didn't show it, whereas Marta could do no wrong. He doted on her.'

'Is that because she's a woman?'

'Probably,' he admitted with a sigh. 'Just as your father treated you differently to your brothers. I struggled for a long time to live with the double standards and his disapproval of me.'

'And now?'

He shrugged, clenching his teeth together. 'And now he's infirm. For years I wanted to take him aside and demand answers about his treatment of me but now it's too late and I will never know.'

'Can't you ask your mum?'

'There isn't any point,' he dismissed. 'My mother always turned a blind eye to it. She turns a blind eye to anything that can be construed as negative. When I left home and set up on my own, her only concern was that I wasn't going to do anything that would bring shame on the Cazorla name.'

'That's a huge assumption you're making about her,' Charley said softly. 'She might surprise you.'

'We'll see,' he said, non-committal. 'The reason I've shared this with you is because if we're going to have any kind of lasting future, we need to always be honest with each other. If you'd been honest about your feelings before, I would have understood, but I'm not a mind-reader.'

A wary, almost frightened expression came into her eyes. 'What do you mean about having a "lasting future"?'

'If we talk and keep the lines of communication open, then these problems won't occur again.'

'You make it sound like we're getting back together properly.'

'Would that be such a bad thing?' he asked in a much calmer tone than he felt. Ever since La Tomatina he'd experienced an awful sickening in the pit of his stomach whenever he thought of the day they would say goodbye for good. Those couple of days away in Brazil, when he'd called her a dozen times just to hear her voice, had convinced him they had what it took to make a new start. He'd missed her so badly he'd been on the verge of jumping into his jet the first night and demanding to be flown home.

Being with Charley felt very different this time too. Easier somehow. Stripped back.

'Get back together?' she asked in a tiny voice.

'We've proven these past few months how good we can be together with a little compromise and sacrifice on each side. We understand each other a lot better too—you must feel that.'

'And would I still be expected to have a baby?'

He could hear the edge in her voice but couldn't place it.

'*Cariño*, you will make a wonderful mother.' And she would. Whatever motherhood threw at her, she would handle it magnificently.

'Are you *mad*?'

His head reared back at the vehemence of her words.

'I can't believe you're talking like this.' The colour had drained from her face to leave her ashen.

A bang on his window brought them both up short.

He turned to find a man there, gesticulating and hollering abuse at him, and saw that traffic was moving again, had most likely been moving for a good few minutes, all bar the cars stuck behind them.

Raising a hand in apology, he was about to put the car back in gear when Charley opened her door.

'What are you doing?'

'I don't know. Going for a walk. I need to clear my head.'

He heard her words but couldn't comprehend them. 'What are you talking about? It's the middle of the night.'

All the colour that had drained from her face came back in a dark flood that reached into her eyes. Her words were a rush. 'I'm sorry, I'm sorry, but I can't do this again.'

Grabbing her bag, she slipped out of the car and slammed the door with so much force the Lotus shook.

Raul stared at her rapidly retreating figure, his heart thumping, something sharp tearing at his throat.

What the hell had just happened?

It took a few heartbeats before the shock of her reaction dislodged and his body unfroze.

He unbuckled his seat belt, jumped out and, ignoring the dozens of angry drivers honking and waving their fists at him, slammed his own door shut.

For a moment he couldn't see her and there were seconds when his heart seemed to stop with the panic of it all. Then he spotted her, already far in the distance in the middle of a crowded pavement.

Charley slipped through the crowds and into a narrow side street where cars were banned, not knowing and not caring where she was going. All that mattered was escaping…

A hand grabbed her arm. Her throat opened to scream but then she saw it was Raul who had hold of her.

She yanked out of his grasp. 'Raul, please, leave me be. I want to be on my own.'

'It's dark—it isn't safe to be out here on your own.'

People shuffled past giving them curious glances.

Raul muttered something and tried to steer her away from the middle of the street. She shied away from his touch.

Under the dim light of the streetlamp, she watched him run his fingers through his hair, his face a dark mask of grimness.

'What is *wrong* with you?' he asked roughly.

'Everything!' And with that, the tears came, not huge sobs or little wails, but a sheet of water pouring out from her eyes over which she had no control. 'Don't you see? Nothing's changed. How can you even *think* we should get back together on a permanent basis and have little Cazorlas when everything that drove us apart in the first place is still there? How could we bring babies into a marriage like that? How can we *ever* bring a baby into a marriage like that?'

'But it isn't the same. We've been better together this time. You know that as well as I do.'

'But that's because we've known it's only temporary.'

He held his hands aloft in an imploring manner. 'It could be for ever this time.'

'We spent *three years* together thinking it was for ever and, you're right, it was all a lie. I was so desperate to meet your expectations of perfection that I lost sight of who I was, and that person is not someone who fits into your world.'

'I have *never* expected perfection from you.' His breathing had become ragged. 'When I met you I lived in a bubble. All my life had been spent in it, a life of wealth and privilege where the most important thing was to keep up the public face. You were the first person outside of that bubble that I noticed. I fell for you the first moment I saw you. All I wanted to do was scoop you up and pull you into the bubble with me and protect you. Can you understand that?'

'Yes, I can, but can't you understand that your bubble suffocated me? I wanted so desperately to make you proud, to be the perfect wife, to hold my own beside you, to give you the beautiful mini Cazorlas we both wanted—and I *did* want them too, I really did, but I needed to find my self-respect first. I never found it with you because the pressure of living up to the perfection of your life was just *too much*.'

The walls of the surrounding buildings seemed to close in on her, crowding her, squeezing her, like creatures from the horror film her fairy-tale marriage had turned into.

She gazed at him, feeling an almost unbearable sadness loom down on her. He looked haggard, as if he'd been told his entire fortune had been lost for ever.

'Raul, your whole life is about perfection. Perfect business, perfect house, perfect car, perfect wife, perfect *everything*. Perfect, perfect, perfect. Look at the new centre for Poco Rio—when it's done it will be perfect and that will be down to *you*.'

She wiped the tears away only to find a fresh torrent pouring down. 'I'm sorry. We're just too different, don't you see that? What we had should never have been more than a summer fling. I can't do it. I can't live that life again. I can't live permanently with *you* again.'

God forgive her, she knew she was being unfair and cruel but fear had caught her in its grip so tightly she would have said anything to relinquish it.

And Raul…forget losing his fortune, he looked as if he'd had all the stuffing knocked out of him.

'Answer me this,' he said, his voice hollow. 'If you don't want me, what *do* you want?'

That brought her up short.

'I don't know. All I know is I don't want to lose sight of who I am again. I just want to be *me*, Charley.' She raised her shoulders and stared at him. 'I want to be happy.'

'And you don't think you can be happy with me?'

'No. I can't be happy with you.'

A shudder ran through her at the same time his face blanched.

She wished she could take it back, all her words, or soften them somehow. But she couldn't. The words wouldn't form.

Raul shoved his hands in his trouser pockets and straightened, visibly composing himself. 'If that's how you feel, there's no point in prolonging this conversation any further. I'll drive you home'

'To my house here?'

He gave a sharp nod, not looking at her. 'If that is what you want.'

'I think that would be for the best.'

On shaking legs, Charley walked back to the Lotus, which was still abandoned in the middle of the road, head-lights still beaming.

Not a single word was exchanged until they pulled up onto her small driveway, the outside lights switching on automatically and bathing them in colour.

His gaze fixed ahead, Raul said, 'I'll arrange for your stuff to be couriered back to you.'

'Thank you.'

'And I'll get Ava to liaise with you about the cruise fundraiser.'

All she managed was a nod, her throat so tight it felt as if she were choking.

When she got out of the car she shut the door softly, sending a silent apology for all the times she'd slammed it in anger.

Don't look back. Don't look back.

She fumbled in her bag for her door key, having a moment of panic as she wondered if she'd taken it out at some point over the past few months. Her fingers gripped on the cold metal…

'Charley.'

She looked back to see Raul standing by his door. 'The new centre… It was you, not me. Everything it is and everything it will be is because of you.'

It wasn't until she stepped into her home and locked the front door that her legs gave way.

He'd called her Charley.

Back to the wall, she slid onto the floor, curled into a ball and sobbed so hard her broken heart shattered all over again.

Raul let himself into the villa and threw his keys on the sideboard.

The house sat in silence, the staff having long retired for the night.

He rubbed his temples and headed to the bar. After fixing himself a neat Gin de Mahón, he sat on a stool, used the remote to turn the television on, and flicked through the sports channels until he found the highlights of the evening's La Liga games.

Sipping at his drink, he concentrated on watching Barcelona demolish Celta Viga. There were some good goals to enjoy and ordinarily he would have been cheering his home team on. Football. His guilty pleasure.

Tonight, though, he was distracted. Something in his trouser pocket was digging into the top of his thigh. He should pick it out.

Instead, he waited for the adverts to finish, swallowed his drink and poured himself another.

The damn thing still dug into him.

With a grimace, he shoved his hand into the pocket and fished the small square box out. Without looking at it, he stuck it on the bar and shoved it away from him. He heard it slide across the marble.

Another game had started. He had no idea which teams were playing.

His eyes kept flitting to the box, still in its wrapping paper. It had landed right at the edge of the bar, part of it overhanging.

When he next picked up his glass his hand had gone clammy. All his skin had dampened, as if he'd caught a fever of the flesh his brain hadn't registered. Just as he thought it, his forehead began to burn and pound and his stomach contracted.

I've eaten something that doesn't agree with me.

But he hadn't eaten. Charley had wanted to leave before they'd really started on their first course.

Charley...

He was off the stool and reaching for the box before he could stop himself. Feeling as if his heart could burst through his ribcage, he ripped the wrapping paper off and popped the lid open.

For a moment he couldn't see for the film that had formed over his eyes. He blinked it away and stared at the contents of the box. The longer he stared, the greater the nausea formed inside him until he could bear it no more and, using all his strength, threw the box at the optics behind the bar, hitting the vodka, the power behind the throw enough to smash the bottle.

He laughed as the smell of alcohol immediately filled the space, was still laughing when he swallowed his Gin de Mahón in one and threw the empty glass at the bottle of single malt whisky. Only the glass smashed.

The laughter died as quickly as it had formed as he surveyed the shattered glass around him.

He couldn't make her happy.

All his attempts to protect her had backfired. He'd suffocated her.

All Charley saw when she reflected on their marriage was unobtainable levels of perfection she didn't believe she could reach. Just as he'd always known he would never be able to reach the levels of perfection his own father had demanded of him.

He clutched at his hair so tightly small strands were locked between his fingers when he pulled them away.

Had he really become his father?

All he'd wanted was to please her and make her happy but all he'd done was drive her away just as his own father had driven *him* away.

The happy ending he'd envisaged for them and had dared hope could be a reality had been cut out from beneath him.

He couldn't make her happy. She didn't want for ever with him.

Holding onto the bar to steady himself, he breathed deeply.

It would pass, he told himself. It had passed last time, it would pass again.

But the pain…

It was intolerable.

The shattered glass was nothing compared to the shattered mess that was his heart.

CHAPTER THIRTEEN

CHARLEY FLOPPED ONTO her sofa and buried her face in her hands.

She didn't think she'd ever felt so exhausted. It wasn't even as if she'd had a particularly busy day. She'd worked at Poco Rio but it hadn't been strenuous, not like some days there could be. She'd then had dinner at her mum's house as her grandma's hip was much improved. They'd had a microwave meal for two, just like the old days.

She should be happy. She had a roof above her head, food in her belly, her mum back on her doorstep and the new centre was progressing nicely, the fundraising cruise was days away...

Oh, but she was going to have to see Raul.

She'd debated not attending, but when she'd told Ava she thought she should stay away Ava had clearly ratted her out to the boss because she'd received a terse email from Raul saying that if she didn't attend he would call the whole thing off.

The email had ended with a postscript: Charley, this is a result of your hard work. Enjoy it, please—you've earned it.

His words had played in her mind since she'd received them.

He'd addressed her as Charley.

He'd also called her that from his car.

Oh, but she *missed* him, a pain like nothing she'd experienced before, not even when their marriage had fallen apart the first time.

She'd spent over two months practically glued to his side. In that time they'd spent only two nights apart, when he'd travelled to Brazil. Right before she'd left him a second time...

Her head began to swim. All the thoughts and feelings she'd studiously avoided and denied these past few weeks crowded in on her with a force that could no longer be ignored.

Was it coincidence she'd broken their relationship on the very day her dad had stood her up again, on her birthday, and after she'd spent two restless nights missing Raul, imagining all the beautiful women who would be on his radar?

Could she...?

Was it possible...?

She straightened.

Was it possible she'd sabotaged their relationship deliberately, out of fear? Because Raul had been right, this time round, once they'd got over their loathing of each other and started to forgive the past, their relationship had been better than she could have dreamed. It had been everything she could have wanted. *Raul* had been everything she could have wanted. They'd been completely at ease with each other. Honest. Without pretence. Equals.

And she'd thrown it all away.

What the *hell* was wrong with her?

Was she really going to let *fear* ruin the rest of her life?

Was she really going to let Raul pay for the sins of her father? Because surely that was where it all originated? A lifetime of feeling replaceable had crept into her psyche and made her believe it to be gospel. Rather than wait for

Raul to leave her for someone more suitable, someone less replaceable, she'd run away.

But he didn't *want* someone more suitable.

He wanted *her*.

He loved *her*.

She sat up straight, suddenly as certain of something as she'd ever been in all her life.

Raul loved her with all her imperfections.

She jumped to her feet, bouncing, then slumped back down as another thought occurred to her.

He might love her but she'd hurt him badly. His pride was enormous and she'd wounded it, not once, but twice.

He might not want to listen to her. Even if he did listen, he could still walk away.

Oh, get some backbone, she snapped at herself. *If he walks away it'll be nothing less than you deserve. You'll still live.*

Better to try than spend the rest of her life wondering what if.

But before she could do *anything*, she realised there was something that needed to be taken care of first.

She'd spent the years of their marriage searching for her self-respect. Somewhere in their short second time together, she'd found it. She didn't know where or when but it had nestled inside her. And now she needed to claim it. Until she claimed it and embraced it, she would never be free to love Raul properly, as he deserved to be loved, and nor would she be free to accept his love as *she* deserved. Because she *did* deserve love. They both did.

Reaching for her phone, she dialled. After a few rings it went to voicemail. She dialled again. The same thing happened.

She would keep trying until her dad answered. After all, he kept his phone on him all the time when he was with her, holding it in his hands while they chatted, or on the table by his cutlery while they ate.

On the fifth attempt her dad answered. He sounded breathless. 'Charley?'

'Hi, Dad.' She took a deep breath and plunged straight in. 'I just wanted to let you know I won't be coming to visit you on Thursday. I'll wire the money you asked for but that will be the last of any money you'll get from me. If you need any more, get a job.'

He spluttered down the line, his words unintelligible.

'I've spent my whole life waiting for you,' she continued. 'I love you very much but I won't wait any more.'

Swiping at her phone to end the call, Charley closed her eyes. After a few moments she opened them and expelled a long breath.

That had felt good. Sad, but good.

How could her father or *anyone* respect her if she didn't respect herself?

Respect had to be earned and that included self-respect.

And as she thought all this, something else struck her, something that made her sit bolt upright and clutch at her heart...

Raul stood in the golden atrium of his new cruise liner, smile fixed to his face, shaking the hands of his guests as they were led through by his crew.

Charley was here somewhere. She'd been aboard since early morning, working with Ava and other members of his executive team to ensure everything was ready.

He hadn't seen her yet.

He hadn't seen her in the three weeks since he'd dropped her back at her tiny house.

He hadn't spoken to her either. Other than the one email he'd felt compelled to send her when Ava had mentioned

Charley was thinking of not coming, there had been no direct contact.

Soon the atrium was full, ladies beautiful in their fanciest dresses, the men dashing in their tuxedos, the heavy scent of perfume and cologne filling the air. He gritted his teeth and forced a welcoming smile as he saw his parents and sister arrive, Marta pushing their father's wheelchair.

He cut through the crowd to them, kissing them all. It was the first time he'd seen them since he'd dropped Charley back at her house in Valencia. He'd cancelled the meal he was supposed to attend at his family's house last weekend.

It was the first time he'd been anywhere other than to work since she'd dropped out of his life.

'Is Charlotte here?' his mother asked.

'She's around somewhere,' he said, his heart clenching as it did every time her name was mentioned. Her name had been mentioned a *lot* in his office, especially by Ava, who seemed to have developed some kind of girl crush on her. Raul found this completely understandable.

'So this thing is for her charity?'

He nodded, not trusting himself to speak.

It was at this moment that they were called into the main restaurant where the first part of the proceedings, the meal, would begin.

Turning away, he followed the crowd to the large board displaying the table plan. As was proper, he'd been placed at the top table with the captain, his parents, sister, and... Where was Charley?

Scanning the other tables, he finally found her name at a door near the entrance, as far from his table as it was possible to get.

He caught Ava's eye and beckoned her over. 'Why has my wife been placed down there?' he demanded to know.

'She's sitting with the children and their families—she thought it best for them to be by the door so if any of them get upset they can take them out and calm them down. She's fabulous, isn't she?' she added reverentially.

Seven children, the same ones who had gone to La Tomatina, plus a couple of others, had been selected to attend with their families. Raul would have had all the children there but for the majority of them it wasn't possible. Rather than being a night they could enjoy, the unfamiliarity and break from routine would have distressed them too much. All their families had been invited, though, as had all the Poco Rio staff and their partners.

He was planning on getting every euro he could from the other guests but for the children, their families and the staff, the night was on him.

He spotted little Karin, the beautiful white-blonde-haired girl who had such an attachment to Charley, and a tall boy in a wheelchair whose name escaped him...

And then he saw her.

She was walking in his direction, deep in conversation with another child's mother.

She must have felt his eyes upon her for she paused and lifted her gaze to meet his.

His chest clenched.

Beautiful. She was beautiful. Glowing.

She was wearing a royal-blue lace dress that fell to mid-thigh and displayed her gorgeous curves, her now even lighter blonde hair loose around her shoulders. She wore black heels, which made her fabulous legs appear even longer.

Even with the distance between them he could see the animation in her eyes.

A tall man he recognised—possibly a famous American singer—stepped in front of her and the contact was broken.

Everyone took their seats.

Wine was poured and the evening began.

Course after course was brought out to them by an army of attentive waiting staff, laughter filling the room, overshadowing the piano player in the corner.

Through it all, through all the conversations he had with the others at his table, Raul's eyes didn't stray far from his wife.

Her table of twelve looked as if they were enjoying themselves immensely, Charley chatting away happily as she ate her food. Every so often she would look over to him and catch his eye and he would feel that pull that had always been there between them, right from the very start. The pull he knew deep down in his soul would never leave him.

He gazed at the children on her table. To her left was the boy in the wheelchair, being fed by his father.

A wave of sadness washed through him to think that boy would never be able to feed himself or do anything for himself. With the sadness came a tiny flicker of pride that he was doing something to make that boy's life a little brighter.

Then his eyes flittered to his father, sitting opposite him in his own wheelchair, being fed by Marta, locked in his own version of hell.

For the first time he felt a wave of compassion for him.

His father had been a hard man. He'd been cruel and demanding of his only son. But no one, not even Eduardo Cazorla, deserved this. And neither did his mother, who could easily have left him in that plush care facility but instead had turned their home and life upside down so he could remain part of the family.

Charley would do the same, he knew. Forget about keeping up appearances, which he knew had played a part in his mother's decision; Charley would never abandon some-one she loved. Not unless she had to—or felt she had to.

While all these thoughts were filtering through his mind, the empty dessert dishes were being cleared away and from the corner of his eye he saw Charley head to the corner of the room where a microphone stand and booth had been set up.

After fiddling with the microphone for a few moments, she tapped it, the thuds of her finger reverberating through the packed room.

'Can everyone hear me?' she asked in Spanish.

Cheers rang round the room.

'Okay, then.' She cleared her throat. When she next spoke, her voice was clear, fluent and full of warmth. 'Before I start the auction, I would just like to say, on behalf of all the children, their families and the staff of Poco Rio, the most enormous thank you to each and every one of you for being here tonight and for spending your hard-earned money on our centre. I promise you, every cent will be spent wisely.'

Even more raucous cheers carried around the room. She stood there beaming, waiting for quiet. 'I would like to extend especial thanks to the wonderful man who made this night happen.'

Suddenly her eyes were on him.

Prickles ran up his spine.

Her smile faded a little but the warmth in her voice grew. 'If it wasn't for Raul, we wouldn't be here and nor would Poco Rio. Please, everyone, raise your glasses. To Raul.'

The word, 'Raul,' echoed around the room, everyone staring at him and drinking to him.

He wanted to smile and accept the toast with good grace but he couldn't do it. It was all wrong. They were toasting the wrong person.

Before he could get to his feet, Charley had started talking again and the auction was up and running.

Once the auction was over, Charley disappeared. He was about to seek her out—he knew she couldn't go far, not with the ship being in the middle of the Mediterranean—when his mother rose and took hold of his father's wheelchair.

'Can't you ask your mum?' Charley had said. He'd dismissed her suggestion out of hand.

But, since he'd driven her out of his life the second time, he'd had time to reflect and suddenly the conversation became imperative.

He followed his parents through to one of the lounges, where he helped his mother settle his father in a quiet corner.

Raul waited until drinks had been served to them and they were all comfortable before talking.

'Why did you just let me walk away from the family business?' he asked, addressing his mother. His father's reaction hadn't been any surprise but it had always played on his mind that his mother's reaction had been negligible.

A look of surprise crossed her Spanish features. 'Could I have stopped you?'

'No.'

'There is your answer.'

He stared at her. 'You didn't even try.'

'But I knew you would be okay whatever you did.'

'How?'

'Because you are just like your grandfather, Nestor.'

'I am?' Nestor had created the Cazorla empire but his name was one seldom mentioned in the privacy of the Cazorla home.

'Of course.' She nodded at her husband, who was gazing at the pair of them, his eyes flashing as if he was desperate to join in with the conversation, then sighed. 'Your father never got on with Nestor any more than he got on with you.'

'But why?' Now he addressed his father directly. 'I always felt as if I were a huge disappointment to you. There were times when I felt as if you hated me and wished I'd never been born. Nothing I did was ever good enough and I need to know why.'

A grunting sound came from his father's throat. His mother patted his knee with a manicured hand, and smiled at Raul. 'I thought you would have worked it out by now; you're an intelligent man. Too intelligent, just like Nestor. He will hate me for saying this but your father had to work hard for what came naturally to you. He struggled with the business. He knew there would come a time when you took over and it would show up the failures he'd made. You intimidated him.'

Now there was a flash of pain in his father's eyes. Suddenly Raul wished he'd chosen to have this conversation out of his earshot. His father couldn't defend himself.

'*I* intimidated *him*? He treated me like *dirt*.' He shook his head and looked at his mother. 'And *you* allowed it to happen.'

'Allowed what to happen? For your father to correct you, as was his right as your father?'

At least she wasn't pretending not to understand.

'My own father was far harder on me than Eduardo ever was with you.' She lifted the sleeve of her arm and showed him the old silvery scar that ran along her biceps. 'My father did this to me in a drunken rage when I was seven. For all his faults as a father, Eduardo never once lifted his finger to you.'

He felt as if he'd been punched. She'd always shrugged it off as a childhood accident. 'I never knew.'

'It was a long time ago when such things weren't spoken of, especially amongst people like my family. Personal problems were kept behind closed doors. We both suffered at the hands of our parents and we tried not to repeat that with you and Marta.'

He laughed without any trace of humour.

'You think your father was hard on you?' his mother said, a sharpness in her voice. 'Nestor would *beat* him when he failed at anything or disappointed him in any way. I accept we didn't always get it right with you but it's those mistakes you will try to avoid when you have your own children. But know, you will make mistakes. We all do.'

The irony almost made him laugh again.

His own children? The only person he wanted to have children with was Charley, and he'd damaged her. Just as his father had damaged him.

Looking back at his father, he could see a whole heap of emotion playing in his eyes and suddenly he knew exactly what the expression meant.

His father wanted to apologise.

A part of him wanted to turn around and walk away and leave the unsaid apology unacknowledged.

Instead, he leant over and covered his father's limp hand and squeezed, then pressed his lips to his cool cheek.

Life had punished his father enough. What kind of man was he to condemn him for eternity when his own actions had driven away the woman he loved?

For the first time he had an understanding of what his own parents had lived through and, while it was too soon to speak of forgiveness, he knew the road to healing—for all of them—had begun.

CHAPTER FOURTEEN

LOT NUMBER FIFTEEN, a week's holiday on Aliana Island, do-
nated by Pascha and Emily Plushenko, went for a hundred
thousand euros—but that was by no means the highest-
selling lot of the evening. That honour went to lot number
twenty-one, a portrait by the artist Grace Mastrangelo,
which sold for a quarter of a million. Those of an artistic
bent nodded wisely and said the winning bidder had got
themselves a bargain.

The numbers were enough to make Charley dizzy. In
one evening, they had raised over a million euros, and that
was without adding the ticket sales. Looking at the dazed
faces of Seve and the other Poco Rio staff, she could tell
they were having trouble processing the figures too.

Now the auction was over and everyone was free to do
as they pleased, be it head to the nightclub to dance or go
to the casino to gamble or to make their way to the theatre where a top musical was being shown with the original cast…or they could head outside as she had done and
stand at the railings looking out at Barcelona in the distance, a mountainous city illuminated magically under the
black sky. She squinted, trying to remember where on the
shoreline their old home had been. When she looked up, a
million stars twinkled down at her.

She inhaled the salty air and tried to capture her thoughts.
What she wanted, more than anything, was to find Raul and

talk to him. She'd planned it all out, everything she wanted to say, but the look on his face after she'd raised the toast to him had stopped her in her tracks. He'd looked furious.

Doubt and her old friend fear had crept back in.

What if he rejected her? What if…?

What ifs didn't matter. She would speak to him before the night was out. She had to.

'May I join you?'

She turned her head with a jolt, her heart immediately racing off at a canter to find him standing there behind her, dazzling in his black tuxedo, carrying two glasses of champagne.

He held one out to her. 'I thought you might be thirsty after all that talking,' he said drily.

'Thank you.' As she took it from him her fingers brushed against his and her stomach somersaulted.

He stood level with her, his body almost touching hers, and gazed out at the same view.

'You were wrong, you know,' he said.

'About what?'

'That speech you made, toasting me. I didn't deserve that. You did.'

'No…'

'Yes. Without you none of it would have happened. This was your vision, your passion. All I did was put your hard work into motion.'

'But without you doing that it wouldn't have happened.'

'Without you doing all the hard stuff at the beginning there wouldn't have been anything for me to do.'

'We can argue over who should receive the praise all night,' she said softly. 'How about we accept it needed both of us to make it happen?'

A faint smile crossed his face and he raised his champagne flute. 'To teamwork.'

'Teamwork,' she echoed, chinking her flute to his. She didn't drink any of it.

'You look beautiful.'

'Thank you.' She made her voice sound cheerful. 'I couldn't go back to dressing up every day but it's nice to do it for special occasions.'

'You always look beautiful, no matter what you wear.'

A lump formed in her throat.

'I want you to know I've signed the deeds for Poco Rio over to you.'

'But the renovations aren't complete yet.'

He dropped his head with a sigh. 'I should never have done what I did. It was a nasty stunt that I pulled and one I am deeply ashamed of. I just hope you can one day find it in your heart to forgive me.'

'You had your reasons,' she murmured, her head swimming.

'No, I didn't—not any reason that makes sense now I think back on them.' He breathed heavily. 'All it needs is your signature to make it official. You can either drop by the office to sign it or I can arrange for it to be delivered to you, whatever makes your life easier.'

'Thank you,' she whispered.

He shrugged, turning his face back out to the illuminated city in the distance. 'I've been thinking. With the amount of money raised tonight, there's more than enough to fund another Poco Rio. How would you feel about scouting out suitable premises in Barcelona for me?'

'For you?' she asked, confused at the turn of direction.

'I'll pay for the building and any renovations that need doing. The funds raised can pay towards staffing and day-to-day running costs.' He must have caught her dumb silence. 'I'm happy to pay outright for it all, staff costs, upkeep, everything. The money raised tonight has been earmarked for the centre and it's only right it be spent on it, but it can also be used to help other children in the same position. If we keep fundraising we can raise more awareness of what these children are living with and help even more of them.'

'And you want me to help you?'

'I want you to run it all for me. I'll pay you a salary—'

'I don't want a salary.'

'I know but I'll pay it anyway. That's if you choose to accept my offer.'

She opened her mouth, not sure what to say, but he spoke forcefully before she could make a sound.

'Don't make a decision now. Think it over. Let me know when you come to a decision.'

If Charley had felt dazed before, that was nothing to how she felt at that precise moment.

He really did trust her. He truly did believe in her.

'I wish I could turn the clock back.'

Her heart skipped.

Sadness had spread over his handsome features. 'It's that bubble we spoke of before—I'm used to living in it but I never thought of how it would be for someone like you, because you're right, it *is* a different world from the one you knew. I just thought you would adapt and fit in, not thinking that I needed to adapt too. It put—*I* put—so much pressure on you it's no wonder the weight of it was too much. I see you now, living back outside the bubble just as you did when we were apart for those two years, thriving.'

Charley stayed silent, letting him say what was on his mind.

'I know my standards are high. Too high,' he admitted ruefully. 'I spent my whole life having every fault picked over by my father. I was always striving for perfection in

the hope of making him proud and getting one word—
that's all I wanted, one word—of praise from him.'

'Being less than perfect doesn't diminish you,' she said.
'It just makes you human.'

'I know. Being with you has taught me that.' He bent
his head and forked his fingers through his hair. 'That's
what I hate the most about myself. I swore I would never
be like him but in my pathetic attempt to punish you for
not wanting my child and having the nerve to leave me,
I became the very thing I despise the most. Because you
were right—that marriage was no place to raise a child.
Can you ever forgive me?'

She smiled wanly. 'I already have.'

He straightened and brushed a finger down her cheek. 'I
used punishing you as an excuse. The truth was I'd missed
you so much that when the opportunity came to have you
back in my life I grabbed it.' Leaning down, he brushed
his lips to her ear and whispered, 'You're the best thing
that ever happened to me, Charley Cazorla. Whatever you
decide to do in the future, be happy.'

With one last brush of his lips to her own, he stepped
back and turned, placed his champagne flute on a small
fixed table, and walked away.

'I lied,' she blurted out to his retreating figure, shoving
her flute next to his.

He stopped mid-step.

'When you asked if I could be happy with you, I lied.
The truth is the two months we just spent together were
the happiest of my life. The past fortnight without you has
been the most miserable.'

He didn't move, standing as still as the marble statues
that encircled the atrium.

Her confidence almost deserted her but she was determined to plough on to the bitter end. He'd put his heart

on the line two weeks ago and she'd rejected him. Even if he rejected *her*, she needed to say it. She would not spend the rest of her life regretting that she'd let this one chance of happiness slip through her fingers.

'I've been a scared, stupid idiot. I've left you twice now and I wouldn't blame you if you told me to get lost but, Raul…' She took what felt like the deepest breath of her entire life. 'I love you. I love you so much it hurts and I know I don't deserve it but if you ever wonder if it could be third time lucky for us…'

She got no further. Raul spun round and in the blink of an eye had her up in his arms kissing her as if there were no tomorrow.

Joy and relief filling her, she wrapped her arms around his neck and burrowed herself into him.

For an age they stood there, Raul holding her securely, his mouth hot on hers, until he gently placed her back on her feet and clasped her cheeks in his hands to gaze intently into her eyes.

'I thought that was it for us.'

She shook her head and clutched at his tuxedo jacket. 'Never.'

'I thought I'd lost you.'

'Never. My heart has been yours since the day I met you.'

'*Cariño…*' Now Raul was the one to shake his head.

'I love you. Totally.' She smiled and traced her fingers across his jawline. 'That bubble you were talking about? Do you think it's possible to live straddling it? One foot in your world, one foot in mine?'

He laughed, a big, deep roar that filled her with such happiness she just had to kiss him again.

Disentangling himself, he stuck his hand into his trouser pocket and pulled out a small square box. 'This is for you. It was supposed to be your birthday present.'

'What is it?'

'Open it and see.'

She flipped the lid open and immediately her heart jumped into her mouth. Nestled in the box was a white-gold and diamond eternity ring.

'It's beautiful,' she whispered.

'I bought it to show you that my love for you is for ever,' he said, taking it out of the box and sliding it onto her empty ring finger.

It fitted perfectly.

'See—now you are mine again.'

She beamed, happiness radiating through her.

'*Cariño*, we will build our own bubble to live in,' he said, placing a reverential kiss to her hand, 'and we will love and celebrate all our imperfections in it.'

'You, me and our babies?'

The laughter died, a serious expression forming in his eyes. 'We will have children when you're ready and not a day sooner. I don't care for the perfect family any more— perfect is *boring*,' he added with a crooked grin. 'Our children will be an expression of our love and commitment, nothing else.'

'How does seven months from now sound to you?'

The shock ringing from him was so palpable that Charley was the one to burst into laughter. 'Yes, you wonderful man, you're going to be a father.'

His eyes were so wide she feared they would pop out. 'How?'

'Do you remember that time in your office…?' She laughed again at the widening of his eyes, relieved to have it out in the open, unable to keep the excitement and joy contained. 'I didn't even *think* about using contraception then.'

'Nor did I,' he admitted, looking completely dazed.

'I took the test yesterday so it's early days. I can't tell you how happy I am...' Her happiness dimmed a fraction. 'You *are* happy too, aren't you?'

'Happy? Charley, I've just got the woman I love more than anything in the world back and I've learned I'm going to be a father. Happy doesn't even come close.'

And there they stood on the deck of the ship, smothered in each other's arms and kisses, oblivious to the passengers milling around them, oblivious to the envious smiles at their obvious, deep love for each other.

EPILOGUE

RAUL PLACED THE scissors to the pink ribbon tied across the front door and said proudly, 'I declare the Poco Rio Madrid open.'

This was the third Poco Rio they'd opened; two more were in the pipeline.

Enthusiastic applause rang out from the crowd around him, the happiest face of all that of his beloved wife, who was leaning against his father's wheelchair, tapping her thigh with one hand rather than clapping with both. Her other hand was holding the base of her enormous belly that strained against the maternity dress she wore.

Passing the scissors to the manager Charley had appointed to run this centre, he hurried over to her side, scooping up two-year-old Sofia on his way. Sofia's face was covered in chocolate. He dug a tissue out of his pocket and wiped it as best he could.

It made him laugh to think that three years ago he would have been horrified to have a child so messy.

Marta had an arm around Charley's waist.

Charley grinned at him but there was a pained expression in her eyes. 'You know I said this morning I felt fit to burst?'

He felt his eyes widen. 'Is it time?'

She nodded.

'Give me my granddaughter,' his mother said, bustling through and tugging Sofia from his arms. She held her up in the air and made silly clucking noises at her. Raul debated for all of a second about telling his mother of the chocolate Sofia had been caught scoffing with the little gang of friends she'd made that morning, before wickedly deciding against it.

'Can Sofia go home with you?' he asked, taking Charley's hand. She squeezed it so hard he winced and he swore he could feel the contraction run through her. 'It looks like grandchild number two is on its way.'

His mother's eyes lit up. 'Of course.' Keeping a firm hold on Sofia, who was screaming to be put down, she kissed them both, rubbing a hand over Charley's belly as she did so. Marta looked as if she were about to go into shock with excitement, while Raul's father's eyes were wide with emotion.

Since their talk on the cruise ship, Raul's relationship with his parents had changed greatly and all for the better. Sofia's birth had cemented the new bond between them. His father loved nothing more than having his wriggling granddaughter placed on his lap so she could smother him with sloppy kisses.

'Call my mother,' Charley said, her words coming in little pants. She managed a pained smile. 'I think this one's in a hurry.'

Exactly one hour and thirty-eight minutes later, Mateo Eduardo Cazorla arrived safely into the world. His mother was tired but delirious with happiness. His father was just delirious, unable to decide who to kiss the most—his beautiful wife or his beautiful son. His big sister was fast asleep after crashing with exhaustion from her chocolate overload. Her dreams were filled with all the happiness she'd known since her own birth.

* * * * *

MILLS & BOON®
Hardback – August 2015

ROMANCE

The Greek Demands His Heir	Lynne Graham
The Sinner's Marriage Redemption	Annie West
His Sicilian Cinderella	Carol Marinelli
Captivated by the Greek	Julia James
The Perfect Cazorla Wife	Michelle Smart
Claimed for His Duty	Tara Pammi
The Marakaios Baby	Kate Hewitt
Billionaire's Ultimate Acquisition	Melanie Milburne
Return of the Italian Tycoon	Jennifer Faye
His Unforgettable Fiancée	Teresa Carpenter
Hired by the Brooding Billionaire	Kandy Shepherd
A Will, a Wish...a Proposal	Jessica Gilmore
Hot Doc from Her Past	Tina Beckett
Surgeons, Rivals...Lovers	Amalie Berlin
Best Friend to Perfect Bride	Jennifer Taylor
Resisting Her Rebel Doc	Joanna Neil
A Baby to Bind Them	Susanne Hampton
Doctor...to Duchess?	Annie O'Neil
Second Chance with the Billionaire	Janice Maynard
Having Her Boss's Baby	Maureen Child

MILLS & BOON®
Large Print – August 2015

ROMANCE

The Billionaire's Bridal Bargain	Lynne Graham
At the Brazilian's Command	Susan Stephens
Carrying the Greek's Heir	Sharon Kendrick
The Sheikh's Princess Bride	Annie West
His Diamond of Convenience	Maisey Yates
Olivero's Outrageous Proposal	Kate Walker
The Italian's Deal for I Do	Jennifer Hayward
The Millionaire and the Maid	Michelle Douglas
Expecting the Earl's Baby	Jessica Gilmore
Best Man for the Bridesmaid	Jennifer Faye
It Started at a Wedding...	Kate Hardy

HISTORICAL

A Ring from a Marquess	Christine Merrill
Bound by Duty	Diane Gaston
From Wallflower to Countess	Janice Preston
Stolen by the Highlander	Terri Brisbin
Enslaved by the Viking	Harper St. George

MEDICAL

A Date with Her Valentine Doc	Melanie Milburne
It Happened in Paris...	Robin Gianna
The Sheikh Doctor's Bride	Meredith Webber
Temptation in Paradise	Joanna Neil
A Baby to Heal Their Hearts	Kate Hardy
The Surgeon's Baby Secret	Amber McKenzie

MILLS & BOON®
Hardback – September 2015

ROMANCE

The Greek Commands His Mistress	Lynne Graham
A Pawn in the Playboy's Game	Cathy Williams
Bound to the Warrior King	Maisey Yates
Her Nine Month Confession	Kim Lawrence
Traded to the Desert Sheikh	Caitlin Crews
A Bride Worth Millions	Chantelle Shaw
Vows of Revenge	Dani Collins
From One Night to Wife	Rachael Thomas
Reunited by a Baby Secret	Michelle Douglas
A Wedding for the Greek Tycoon	Rebecca Winters
Beauty & Her Billionaire Boss	Barbara Wallace
Newborn on Her Doorstep	Ellie Darkins
Falling at the Surgeon's Feet	Lucy Ryder
One Night in New York	Amy Ruttan
Daredevil, Doctor...Husband?	Alison Roberts
The Doctor She'd Never Forget	Annie Claydon
Reunited...in Paris!	Sue MacKay
French Fling to Forever	Karin Baine
Claimed	Tracy Wolff
Maid for a Magnate	Jules Bennett

0815 GEN STD HB